From
Despair
to Miracles

Josh's Struggle for Survival

DONALD CABABE

PAGE PUBLISHING, INC.
New York, NY

First originally published by Page Publishing, Inc. 2018

ISBN 978-1-64424-144-8 (Paperback)
ISBN 978-1-64424-145-5 (Digital)

Printed in the United States of America

"Oh no! This can't be happening. Not now, after all these years. Oh no!"

Seventeen-year-old Josh looked for a place to park his sputtering car, thinking the car would die before he found a parking space. A half block away, he saw an empty space. The sign read, "Residents Only." Another block, the car stalled. Josh was in a panic, starting to sweat, his hands were shaking. He turned the ignition saying, "Please start, please." A few seconds of the engine cranking, but it finally turned over. Josh breathed a heavy sigh of relief. Another block, another space . . . and no sign. He pulled in and the engine stalled again. He leaned back on the headrest and simply stared into space feeling totally defeated.

Then the tears came, slowly at first, but in a matter of seconds the tears came cascading down his cheeks, followed by loud and heavy sobbing. About a minute later, the sobbing ceased. Josh's stare slowly turned into a determined look as he clenched his teeth and squinted his eyes. He said out loud, as if he wanted to hear the proclamation himself, "I know what I have to do. It's the only way out, the only solution."

Josh reached into his backpack and pulled out his most prized possession—his only prized possession. He looked at the photo of his Aunt Sue, Uncle John and his two cousins, Jared and Jason. He smiled, and after about thirty seconds he said once again out loud, "Hello Aunt Sue, Uncle John, Jared, Jason. I'm sorry, but I have to tell you this is the last time I'll be talking to you." He paused and the tears began anew.

"I will miss our nightly talks." Pause, the crying begins. "I love you guys so much but I can't take this anymore. I tried, oh god, how I tried for ten long years." Heavy sobbing.

"I'm so sorry, but I know the only way out of this misery is to end it all. I can't go on living this life anymore. I want you to know that I love all of you so very much. So goodbye Aunt Sue, goodbye Uncle John, goodbye Jared, goodbye Jason. I love you."

Josh sat in his nearly broken down car for fifteen minutes thinking about his life and his almost four years with Aunt Sue and Uncle John. They were always there for him, helping him, providing for him, having fun with him.

* * *

Although he lived with his biological parents, they always remained distant to Josh—no love, no guidance, no interaction. They rarely talked to Josh and only did, it seemed, when they were hollering at him or ordering him to do things like cleaning the house, mowing the lawn and anything else they could think of. They didn't work for as long as Josh remembered (He found out later that they were on disability). Every day, all day and night, they would be drinking beer or alcohol and doing drugs. Too often, their friends would join them for their partying (Of course, Josh had to do the post partying clean-up every day). Sometimes there was food in the house, but that was only in the form of cold cuts. Nothing was ever cooked in that house as far as Josh remembered. There were many, many days when there was no food, and Josh had nothing to eat.

After he met Aunt Sue and Uncle John for the first time at age six, it didn't take long for them to determine that his parents were neglecting Josh so they took care of him as much as they could. He would eat dinner at their house as often as he was able to, that is, when he was able to sneak out of the house. Aunt Sue and Uncle John also would buy him clothes and take him places just so he could get away from his house. Their two sons, his cousins Jared and Jason, adored Josh, Jared being two years younger and Jason four years younger than Josh. The three of them did a lot of fun things together playing ball, wrestling around and doing other fun things young boys would do.

Josh's parents were well aware of all that Sue and John were doing for Josh and they resented it and them. For a long time, Josh would hear his parents say mean things about them, and they tried to keep them apart. They saw how Sue and John treated Josh, and whenever his parents told Sue and John to keep away from Josh, Sue and John would simply ignore them. When Josh was about eight years old, the beatings began almost daily . . . not only face slapping, but punches in the arm and stomach, and kicking. Josh spent most nights crying himself to sleep. Josh's father warned him that if he tells anyone they would kill him, and they would also kill Aunt Sue and Uncle John. One day during the beatings, one of the punches landed just below his left eye which resulted in redness in the area and then a black eye. The next day, his Aunt Sue saw him walking home from school. She stopped her car and called for Josh to get in.

In the car, Aunt Sue saw his left eye and said, "Josh, what happened to your eye?"

Josh replied, "Well, uh, um, I fell and hit my face."

"Where did you fall?"

"Uh, um, I fell out of bed and hit the floor."

"Josh, look at me. Tell me what really happened. Did your parents hit you?"

No response from Josh.

Sue hugged Josh and said "Josh honey baby, it's all right, just tell me the truth."

Josh started to cry and said, "Yeah, they hit me, and they hit me all the time. I hate them."

"How long has this been going on?"

"About two years, I think."

"But why didn't you tell me or Uncle John?"

"Because I was scared. They told me if I did they would kill me and you and Uncle John, and I didn't want them to hurt you."

"Josh, don't worry about a thing, and don't tell your parents that you told me, okay?"

"I won't, Aunt Sue."

"Good, we're going home where I'll take care of your eye."

The next day, Sue went to the police station to file a complaint and then to the Child Protective Service. The police told Sue that they would visit Josh's parents and probably issue a citation as well as a warning that if it happens again, they would both be arrested and put in jail. They also said that this is a matter for the Child Protective Service. After Sue filed a complaint with the CPS, she also filled out forms asking for legal guardianship of Josh. Sue was not encouraged by what the police told her, but she was more than encouraged by the CPS. The Social Worker told Sue that they would probably set a date for a hearing for the charges of abuse and neglect, as well as Sue's petition to take custody of Josh. Sue thought it best to not tell Josh what she was doing since she did not want him to be let down if things did not turn out the way she had hoped. The next day the police and CPS agent visited Josh's home. The day after those visits, Josh's world around him came crashing down. His parents told him they were moving and told him to throw all his clothes in paper bags.

Josh asked, "Where are we moving to?"

His father said, "Just shut up and do as you're told." He slapped Josh in the face. Josh started to cry as he put his hand on his face where he had been slapped.

"You worthless piece of scum. Now go to your room and throw your stuff in a bag. From now on things are going to be different with us."

Josh sobbed, "Does Aunt Sue and Uncle John know we're moving?"

His father then punched Josh in the face and Josh landed on the floor and he was crying harder.

"Your precious aunt and uncle moved to California, so you'll never see them again. And I don't ever want to hear their names ever again."

Josh got up, ran to his room and collapsed on his bed and continued crying. Two hours later, Josh was still crying when his father barged into his room. "Get your rear end off the bed. We're leaving NOW." Josh stood up and walked, zombie-like, to the closet and stuffed all he had into two paper bags.

* * *

Josh wiped his face and got out of his car with a look of determination on his face. He leaned against the driver's side door and, for some inexplicable reason, he took out his wallet and counted his money . . . $211. He then let out a mocking chuckle and thought, *Why am I counting my money when I'm going to kill myself?* He put his money away and started to think about how he was going to do the deed. He looked to his left and saw the ocean. He simply stared at it. Maybe. Then he thought of other ways . . . buy a knife? nah, too messy; buy a load of over-the-counter pills? nah, suppose I throw them up; walk in front of a speeding car? nah, not a guarantee. He turned and stared again at the ocean. He said to himself, "I gotta think about this. I'm too tired to think now. I know what to do. I'll get a hotel room, get some rest, and then I'll be able to think better and plan this out. Might as well, I won't be needing money anymore."

He stood up and looked around trying to get his bearings. He was somewhere in Key West where he had never been before. He saw someone walking toward him and when the lady got near, Josh asked, "Excuse me, do you know of a cheap hotel that's nearby?"

The lady thought for a few seconds and said, "Well, there is a resort about two blocks from here. I've never been there, but I hear it's a nice place and that they do have cheap rooms."

"Okay, I'll check it out. Where is it?"

"Go to the next corner and turn right. It's about one block down. The name is Paradox Resort."

"Thanks, ma'am, I appreciate it."

"Good luck."

Josh got his backpack out of the car, locked up and headed for the Paradox. He got to the Paradox, walked in and approached the person behind the counter. The clerk looked at Josh, smiled and said, "Welcome to Paradox. My name is Joan. Can I help you?"

"Do you have a room available, the least expensive?"

"Certainly, the cheapest room is $69, but it's very small and only has a bed in it. You would have to use a common bathroom and shower for men." Joan chuckled and said, "Don't go to the ladies' commons."

"That's not a problem."

"How many nights is this for?"

"Only one."

"Uh, may I ask how old you are?"

Josh thought, *Oh no*, but he lied, "I'm twenty-one."

Joan had a skeptical look on her face, "Sorry for asking. How would you like to pay, credit or cash?"

"Cash. Should I pay now?"

"No, you can pay when you check out, but I do need identification. Do you have a driver's license?"

"Yes, but do you really have to see it?"

Joan looked at Josh, and at his red-from-crying eyes and whispered, "I shouldn't be doing this, but take out your license so I can see your picture, the expiration date and license number. You can put your thumb on whatever it is that you don't want me to see."

"Thank you so much."

Joan whispered again, "Don't order any alcohol in the cafe."

"I promise I won't. I've never had any alcohol."

"I believe you." A pause. "Are you going to be all right?"

"Yes, I will be. I just need to rest and sleep a little."

"Fine. I'll show you to your room and the commons. While we're walking, I'll tell you about our amenities. We have a pool, two Jacuzzis, one indoor and one outdoor, a video room, an exercise room, a sauna, steam bath and a cafe. Here we are, your room is right here, and there's the commons. Have a good rest, and if there is anything I can do for you, let me know."

Josh thanked Joan and walked into his room which seemed the size of a walk-in closet with only a bed in it and no room to walk. He lay down on the bed and thought to himself, *Now what do I do?* He looked at his watch which read 3:15 p.m. He then realized how exhausted he was, more mentally than physically. He started to think of how he was going to carry out his plan but soon drifted off to sleep. The next thing he remembered was awakening in a start, yelling "No, no, no." An obvious nightmare of which he had no recollection.

Josh looked at his watch: 6:20 p.m. The three-hour sleep did little to relieve his mental and emotional anxiety. Although he hadn't eaten since yesterday morning, he didn't feel hungry at all. But he thought maybe eating something would help clear his mind because he had some serious thinking and deciding to do later. So off he went to the cafe, but not before he took out his 'most prized possession' and gazed at it a bit, a slight smile on his face and, of course, more tears from his eyes.

He sat at a table still looking at the photo through his bloodshot eyes. He mumbled, "I love you Aunt Sue." And the tears began to fall again. A customer at the table next to Josh asked, "Are you okay?"

Josh replied rather harshly, "Yeah, yeah, I'm just fine."

"Is there anything I can do to help?"

"No one can help me."

"I'd like to try. I really would like to help you."

Josh snapped back, "Listen, I don't want help from you or anyone. Just leave me alone."

"Sure, sorry for bothering you. But for what it's worth, I would like to help."

A waiter came to Josh's table, and he obviously saw that Josh was distressed. He looked at the customer who tried to talk to Josh. That customer shook his head, definitely sending a message to ignore Josh's condition. The waiter turned to Josh and said, "Hello, my name Brian. Would you like anything to drink?"

"Just water please."

"Right away."

When the waiter returned, he asked, "Would you like to order something to eat?"

Josh, still looking at the photo, looked at the waiter with glazed eyes and a blank look on his face. He said, "Uh, well, uh, do you have soup?"

"We have clam chowder and conch chowder."

"Uh, could you tell me how much it is?"

"A cup is $1.95 and a bowl is $2.95."

"Just a cup of conch chowder please."

With that, the customer sitting next to Josh got up and approached Brian as he was leaving Josh's table. He said to Brian, "Hey Brian, that boy has problems and it's not only money. I tried to get him to talk but no dice."

"That's too bad."

"Listen, don't bring the soup right away. Bring him a cheeseburger, waffle fries and a large coke, and oh yeah, bring his soup with the burger. Tell him the bill and tip have been taken care of and charge it to my room. Brian, he doesn't need to know who's paying. And make sure he eats."

"How am I supposed to do that?"

"I don't know. Bribe him, threaten him, force him. If you have to, tie his hands up and force feed him."

The customer then left the cafe.

When Brian set down on Josh's table a very oversized cheeseburger, waffle fries, large coke, and oh yeah, the cup of conch chowder, Josh looked shocked and panicky. He said, "Wait, I didn't order this. What are you doing? I only ordered soup."

Brian answered, "I know you didn't, but it's bought and paid for. So enjoy."

"But . . . who . . . why?" Suddenly Josh got it. It had to be the guy who tried to talk to him.

"I'm not at liberty to tell you who, but please eat. I was told to bribe you, threaten you or force you. Or if I had to, tie your hands up and force feed you."

"You don't have to tell me who it is. I know who did this. Do you know the guy who was sitting here?"

"I know him. He's been coming here for years. He one of our best customers and one of the nicest people you'll ever meet. He once wrote me a glowing recommendation. Great guy. Tell you what. You eat all your food and then I'll . . ."

"Yeah? What?"

"Just eat. I'll be back."

As Josh began eating he realized he was ravenous. He kept thinking about what the customer said and what Brian said about him. Josh thought, *It doesn't matter, he can't help me, no one can. But he did seem like a nice guy and I treated him like crap. I'll find him and apologize. Then I'll get on with my plan.*

When Josh was done eating, Brian came to the table and said, "I'm glad you ate. How was it?"

"Great. You were going to tell me where I can find the guy who bought this."

"Well, I didn't exactly say that."

"But you said . . . "

"I said I can't *tell* you, but watch closely." Brian lifted up his hand and raised his index and middle fingers, put them down, then raised his index finger, put it down, then raised all four fingers.

"Huh?" Brian repeated his signals and then looked toward the rooms.

"Oh, I get it. Thanks, Brian." Josh rushed to the rooms to look for room 214.

"Room 208, 210, 212 . . . must be the next one." Josh got near the room and saw his benefactor sitting outside his room where there was a small round table and two chairs.

When the guy saw Josh, he said with a smile on his face, "Well hello, nice seeing you again."

Josh replied, "You didn't have to do that you know. I have money."

"I guess you figured it out. I know I didn't have to, but I wanted to. I hope you're not angry with me."

Josh said, "Can I sit down?"

"Of course, please do."

"I'm not mad or anything. You're the one who should be mad because of how I treated you downstairs. I came to thank you for being so kind and for doing what you did. By the way, I did eat the burger and most of the fries and Brian didn't have to tie me up and force feed me." The guy laughed and Josh gave a slight grin. "But mostly, I want to apologize for how I behaved and how I snapped at you. It's just that I have a lot of things going on right now, not that that's an excuse. I'm really sorry because what you heard is not the type of person I am. I guess I owe you big time."

"You didn't have to apologize, and I know that is not who you are. You strike me as a very nice and respectful young man. Why don't we start all over and make believe downstairs didn't happen? Hello, my name is Mark. It's nice to meet you . . . your turn."

"Uh, my name is Josh." They shook hands.

"Josh, I could see you have a serious problem and I'll tell you again, I really want to help you."

"I don't understand. Why would you want to help me? You don't even know me."

"Let me just say, I've met and dealt with many young people your age who had serious problems."

"Yeah, but nothing like mine I bet. But where did you deal with these kids? Were you some kind of social worker?"

"No, I was a high school teacher for many years, and I worked with probably hundreds of students with problems."

"I don't get it. You think I am a nice kid and that I have serious problems. How do you think that?"

"I'm pretty good at reading young people. For example, let me guess about some of your problems. Tell me if I am wrong. I'm guessing you left home, probably today. And that you had a pretty poor home life with parents who didn't care about you, probably abusive, either mentally or physically, probably both. How am I doing so far?"

Josh just stared at Mark with his mouth wide open. After a few seconds, he said, "How did you know all that?"

"Lucky guess, I suppose. Listen Josh, I know that you don't know me, and I suspect you have difficulty trusting other people and that's understandable. I don't like to talk about myself so I have an idea. Do you know what a memoir is?" Josh nodded yes. "I want you to take my laptop and read two sections of my memoir. I'll give you the page numbers. After you read it, I think you'll find out who I am and why I want to help."

"You'd trust me with your computer?"

"Of course. Will you read it tonight?"

"Yes, but I have to check out tomorrow."

"Oh? Do you have any plan of action?"

With his head down, Josh slowly and hesitantly said, "I thought all day about that . . . and I decided to . . ."

"Decided what?"

"Nothing really, nothing important."

"Okay. Josh, you said before that you owe me big time." Josh nodded his head. Mark continued, "There is something I want you to do. I want you to tell me some of your problems. I promise I'll tell no one. I want to see if there is something I can do to help. Besides, talking about your problems may take a big load off your shoulders. If tomorrow you want to take off, I'll say nothing. You have nothing to lose and maybe, just maybe, a lot to gain."

"I don't know if I want to talk about it. I've been thinking about nothing else for weeks. I'm so sick and tired of thinking about it. It's so bad that I have trouble sleeping."

"That is precisely why I want you to talk about it. By doing this, it's like putting your problems in the past tense. As I said before, talking about it just may take a big load off your shoulders. How about starting, and if you can't continue, then stop. What do you say?"

"Do you really think it will help?"

"Yes, I do, I really do Josh."

Josh looked like he was in deep thought and after about thirty seconds he said, "Okay, I'll try it. But could we do it in your room. I don't want anyone to listen."

Once inside the room, Josh said, "Whoa, what a nicc room. My room is so small the bed barely fits. Wow, look at the bathroom. I have to use a common bathroom and shower."

Mark said, "Make yourself comfortable. There's soda in the mini-fridge so whenever you want, help yourself. Listen Josh, take your time and say anything you want. Take a deep breath and think to yourself, 'This is something I have to do' . . . or something like that."

Josh took a deep breath and Mark could swear that the look on his face slowly changed from fear and weakness to one of strength and determination. After nearly a minute, Josh began, "I'll give you a short version rather than a blow by blow account. So here goes. As far back as I can remember, maybe age five or six, my parents hardly ever talked to me and only did so when they told me, or I should say ordered me to do something, or when they yelled at me for making a mistake or doing dumb things. For food, the only thing I ever ate was cereal sometimes and cold cuts. Never had a cooked meal at that house, and there were many times when I had nothing to eat."

"I don't know how old I was when I realized my parents were drinking all the time and doing drugs, so I was happy when they left me alone. I was really scared of them. I think I was about six years old when my Aunt Sue came to our house. I didn't even know who she was. I'll never forget that day. She was so beautiful. and she was smiling at me. She came over to me and told me she was my aunt. She said 'Give me a big hug.' I didn't know what she meant so I stood there. She put her arms around me and hugged me. I hugged her back. I had never been hugged before and it felt so good. She told me that she and her family moved into town because my uncle was starting his own business nearby. She told me she had two sons that she wanted me to meet them. This was the first time I ever felt good about anything."

"From that day on, I saw her and her family fairly often. I guess she sensed that things were not right in our house so she let me spend time at her house. I ate dinner with them when I could. God, I was so happy for the first time in my life. I felt like I now had a family. I looked at Aunt Sue and Uncle John as my real parents. But lots of times, my parents wouldn't let me go see Aunt Sue."

"I knew my parents resented the fact that I was spending so much time with Aunt Sue because they told me that many times.

They told me not to go there anymore, so when I could I used to sneak out to go Aunt Sue's house. Then when I was about eight years old they started hitting me almost every day, slapping my face, punching me in the stomach or on my arms, often kicking me. I learned soon enough to wear long sleeve shirts so no one would see the bruises." Josh paused and the tears began to fall.

Mark said, "Do you want to stop?"

"No, I want to get through this. I'll be okay," Josh continued, "I never told Aunt Sue about the beatings. That was because I was so afraid to because my parents told me I'd better not or they would kill us all. Then one day, their face slaps turned into punches so I ended up getting a black eye. When Aunt Sue saw it, she asked if my parents did that and I said yes. I told her all the things they did. She was furious and said she would do something about it. She asked me if I wanted to stay at her house that night, but I said I better not because I was afraid they would hurt Aunt Sue and Uncle John."

"The next day, a policeman came and asked me about the eye. I forgot what I told him. Then a lady showed up and asked me the same question. I think she was a social worker."

"After they left, I heard my father on the phone saying something like he needed those papers today and that he would pay $10,000. I had no idea what he was talking about." Josh then repeated what his father said about moving and that Aunt Sue moved to California. That was the last time he saw Aunt Sue. He said the next six years were like hell for him and that he was focused only on surviving and getting away from his so-called parents.

Sensing that Josh was becoming upset, Mark said, "That's enough Josh, I got the picture. Let me ask a couple of questions. First, how did you get to Key West?"

"I drove."

"Where did you get the car? Did you buy it?"

"No, my parents had two cars and my mother rarely used hers. I knew I was finally leaving that house, I was seventeen at the time, so when they were sleeping or probably passed out, I searched around and found the title to her car and took it. I also found in their room a stack of money and a load of drugs, marijuana and I guess cocaine, and I don't know what else. I also took my birth certificate. So when I was ready to leave, I forced them to sign over the car to me. I told them if they didn't, I would call the police and tell them all about their drugs. They signed it over."

"Do you now know what the papers were?"

"Oh yeah. I found out that they changed my name and had, I guess, a forged birth certificate. They used that one to enroll me into a new school. Keep in mind, at that time I was only ten years old, well almost eleven, so I didn't understand what was going on. So my name was Josh Armstrong, then it became Greg Smith."

"Okay, let me get something straight. The day after your Aunt Sue saw your black eye, both the police and someone from Child Protective Service came to your home. And that same day, the papers talk on the phone, and the day after that, they told you they're moving and that Aunt Sue moved to California."

"That's right. Why?"

"Just thinking. Is Aunt Sue's last name Armstrong?"

"No, it's Brennan."

"What city did you and Aunt Sue live in?"

"Browning, Florida. About one half hour from Fort Lauderdale."

"Did she live close to you? And do you remember the street she lived on?"

"She lived about a mile from us. The street? I'm not sure but I think the name was some type of a tree. Why did you ask that?"

"Just curious. I guess I was just testing your memory. Just one more question. How or why did you end up at the Paradox."

"Well, as soon I drove into Key West, the car started acting up. It was sputtering and backfiring while I drove and every time I stopped for a red light or something, it stalled. So I looked for a parking space and found one about two blocks from here. I don't know what to do with the car."

Mark thought for about thirty seconds, then said, "I think you've had enough for tonight. It's now nine fifteen so I want you to take the computer and read those two sections. Try to get some sleep tonight. Take a couple sodas with you to your room in case you get thirsty. I want you to meet me in the cafe in the morning at about eight thirty, no later. Before you check out. Is that okay?"

"I'll be there eight thirty, sharp. By the way, my room number is 104 in case you do bed checks."

Mark thought that Josh's humorous comment was a very positive development. He laughed and said, "Great. There's one last thing. I need you to promise me something. But let me tell you . . . to me a promise is like a sacred vow. So don't promise unless you really mean it. I want your promise that you won't do anything foolish tonight."

"What do you mean?"

"Josh, I think you know exactly what I mean. You said before that you made some type of decision after your car broke down. I'm sure I know exactly what that decision was."

With a shocked and scared look on his face, Josh said, "How could you . . . oh god, oh god." Tears started to trickle from his eyes. "I'm so sorry. Mark, I'll promise under one condition."

"What's that?"

"That you give me a hug."

"Gladly."

After Josh left, Mark quickly called the front desk. Since he didn't have his computer, he needed to get the area code for Browning. He got it, pulled out his cell phone and said anxiously, "Aunt Sue, please be listed. Make my job easy. Be listed." He called Browning information and asked for the number of either John or Sue Brennan in Browning. He said, "I'm not sure of the address but I think the street name is some kind of tree." He nervously paced around the room while he waited.

"Sir, there are many Brennan's listed. Let's see, Browning, Browning." Pause. "No John Brennan. Let me look for Sue." Pause. "Oh, I have an S. Brennan on Sycamore Ave. Is that a tree?"

"*Yes*, yes it is. Right now it's a beautiful tree as far as I am concerned. May I have the number?"

After Mark hung up the phone he impulsively yelled out, "Yes . . . Yes" as he pumped his fist into the air. Mark thought, *Should I call now?* He looked at his watch . . . 9:32 p.m. Probably too late. Who knows if they slept early. He decided it was better to wait until tomorrow.

Mark walked into the lobby at seven fifty-five the next morning. He was waiting for Alan who started his shift at the front desk at eight. Mark always dealt with Alan who always goes out of his way to help or handle any problems. Two minutes later, Alan arrived and when he saw Mark, he greeted him with a smile, "Good morning, Mark. Is there anything I can do for you?"

Mark said he really hoped so. Mark began explaining Josh's dilemma without going into detail. He simply told Alan that Josh had some serious problems and that he was trying to help him out.

He told Alan that Josh is scheduled to check out today and that he wanted to pay for the room now. He then told Alan that he wanted to reserve a better room, one with a bathroom and shower. Alan said no problem. He went to his computer and went to work. Alan reserved room 118 and he said it was a very nice room. He asked Mark how many nights he should book it for. Mark thought for a few seconds and said to book it for three days and if that changes, he'd let Alan know. Mark then paid for Josh's current room.

Mark told Alan about Josh's car problem and asked if he knew of a mechanic in the area. Alan said he knew a good mechanic who was also a good friend, and his shop was only about a mile away. Mark asked him to call to see if he had time today to work on the car. Alan made the call and started to talk to the mechanic. He hung up the phone and said it was all set, the mechanic was expecting Mark. He told Mark the mechanic's name was Alex. He then said that to get there, "Go South on Whitestone Road which is the street that the Paradox is on, drive about one mile and when you see the Hess station, pull in there. This is where Alex does his work." Mark thanked Alan and headed to the cafe to wait for Josh.

At eight twenty-five, Josh walked in with his backpack and the laptop. He sat down and said, "Wow, I could not believe what I read."

The waiter came by and asked if they were going to have breakfast. When Josh said not really, Mark ordered him an omelet.

Mark said, "Were you able to sleep last night?"

"Oh yeah, that's the best I slept in a long time. Fell asleep around eleven thirty and woke up about seven thirty. I only used the common bathroom. I didn't want to share a shower with other guys. But tell me, is what I read all true?"

"Every word, no exaggerations."

"Whoa, you are amazing. I wish I had a teacher like you. My favorite part was the 'Friend' section and I loved all those quotes. I read everything two times last night and again this morning. Wow."

Mark asked, "Now do you know why I want to help you?"

"Yeah I get it, but I don't think there's much you can do. But I do appreciate everything you've done so far. The last time someone did something nice for me was when Aunt Sue . . ."

"Josh, let's not think about all that stuff now. Let's think about going forward."

"Yeah, you're right. I'm sorry. I'll try. Wait." Josh then put his head down, chin to chest. "I'm ready."

"Ready for what?"

"To be bopped. I want to become one of your dumb kids."

Mark laughed and lightly bopped Josh on his noggin. "There, you are now officially my new dumb kid." They both laughed but Josh was actually beaming. He looked happy and proud of his new title.

Mark thought to himself, *Fantastic, more progress.*

The waiter brought their breakfast and they chatted while they ate. Josh said in between bites, "Don't forget I have to check out when we're done."

Mark asked, "Any thoughts as to where you'll be heading?"

"Obviously I have to head north, so I think I'll go to Miami." After Mark asked why, Josh continued, "Well, I have $211. After I pay for my room, I'll still have about $130. So when I get to Miami, I'll try to find a cheap room, maybe at a YMCA, and then I'll look around for a job. I won't need too much money to get by."

Mark was doing everything he could to avoid laughing since Josh didn't know of his plan. He said, "Aren't you forgetting something?"

When Josh asked what, Mark said, "Your car."

"Whoa, I forgot about that. I know it won't make it to Miami so I'll take a bus or something. But what can I do with the car?"

"Well, you can always junk it."

"Yeah, maybe I can get money for it. Thanks for thinking of it."

"Tell me Josh. Do you think you can trust me?"

"Absolutely. I mean you've been so nice to me and after reading your memoir . . . I really do trust you."

"Great." After he signed for the bill, Mark said, "Josh, I have to go someplace to meet someone. Could you give me a ride? It's only about a mile from here."

"Yes, but I don't know if the car will make it that far."

"I'm sure it will . . . let's go."

As they walked through the lobby Josh asked if he should check out now. Mark said he can do it when they get back. He told Josh to check his backpack instead of lugging it around. After they got in the car, Josh was shocked that it started right away. They got on Whitestone, drove for three blocks and had to stop for a red light. The car stalled.

"Uh-oh." That came from Josh. Josh turned the key to try to start the car and after a few seconds it did start. "Whew." Josh again.

They proceeded and were fortunate enough to not hit any more red lights. When Mark saw the Hess station he told Josh to slow down and pull into the station. He then told him to drive up to the bays.

Mark and Josh got out of the car and went toward the bay area. When a mechanic saw them, he approached them and said, "You must be Mark. I'm Alex."

"I'm happy to meet you Alex. This is Josh, and this is his car. I hope we're not causing a problem by coming on such short notice."

"Not a problem. We're slow anyway. And even if I was busy, since it was Alan who called, I would have dropped whatever I was doing. He's a close friend and a great guy. So tell me what the problem is?"

Mark told Josh to explain to Mark what problems he was having with car. Josh said, "Well, I drove into Key West yesterday, and the car began sputtering and backfiring. Then whenever I had to stop for a traffic light or something, it stalled. Just now, we drove about a few blocks and we hit a red light and it stalled. The engine is still sputtering and backfiring."

Alex said, "Could be a couple of things, but I'm sure your carburetor is one of the problems. Could I call you in about an hour to give you the bad news," he chuckled when he said that, "and an estimate, but I'll give you my Alan special discount."

Mark gave him his cell number and said, "Alex, could you check everything in the engine and his brakes. He may have a long ride ahead." Mark looked at the tires and said, "He'll need new tires. Take a look at his spare as well."

As Mark and Alex were speaking, Josh was standing there wide-eyed with his mouth agape. As each spoke, Josh's head turned rapidly back and forth to the one speaking. He could not believe what he was hearing.

"I'll check everything out and give you a call."

"Thanks a lot, Alex." Josh added, "Yes, thank you, sir."

As Mark and Josh walked away, Mark said, "Let's walk back, it's not too far."

Josh said, "Are you crazy? I can't let you do that. It's way too much."

"I can and I will. How do you propose to stop me?"

"Please, when he calls tell him you changed your mind and that I want to junk the car."

"No way, José. I'm going to do it. Besides, it will help solve one of your problems."

Josh stopped and looked at Mark. With tears in his eyes he said, "Thank you Mark, you are the best."

He then gave Mark a big hug. "If the car can be fixed, then I can leave for Miami tonight."

"We'll see."

They continued walking toward the hotel while Josh told Mark more about his life. When they arrived, they both thanked Alan and told him what a nice guy Alex is and that Alex spoke highly of Alan.

Josh asked Alan, "Can I check out now?"

Alan said, "You're already checked out and your room is paid in full." He looked at Mark with a grin.

"Huh? But . . . how . . . who." Suddenly, it dawned on him and he turned to Mark, "Oh my god, Mark. You can't do this. Please let me pay." Mark looked at Alan and nodded.

Alan spoke up and said, "And here is the key to your new room. Room 118. This one has a bathroom and shower."

Josh looked stunned, but Mark said to him, "Come on, Josh, let's get you settled in your new room and then we'll talk." Alan gave Josh his backpack. After they both thanked Alan, they headed to Josh's bathroom-and-shower-included room.

When they entered the room, Josh said, "Whoa, this is a nice room. I can even walk around a little. Wait, I gotta check out the bathroom. Whoa! It sure beats a closet room."

"Mark, I don't know how I can ever repay you for what you're doing for me." He sat on his bed with tears starting to form.

"Josh, I'll tell you what you can do for me. Just stay being the nice person you are and focus on your future. You've fought and overcame many problems, always looking forward to a better life. Build up a determination that you *will* make it and that you *will* be successful. That's what you can do for me."

Josh jumped up and hugged Mark and said, "I will, Mark. I promise you. And that's a sacred vow."

"Okay, it's now nine twenty. What do you want to do today?"

"I don't care. Anything you want to do."

"How about if we hang out at the pool for a while and then later make use of some of the amenities . . . the sauna, Jacuzzi, game room. Just a day of relaxation and fun."

"Sounds great."

"Do you have shorts or something for the pool? If not, we can go out and buy some."

"I have a couple pairs of shorts I can use."

"Great. Let's do it. I'll go get changed, and since you didn't shower this morning, take one now before you stink up the place. I'll meet you at the pool."

At the pool as they were lying in lounge recliners taking in the sun, Josh asked, "Say, what was all that talk this morning about junking my car when you knew we were going to a mechanic?"

"I was just going along with you. I thought it was amusing especially the bit about taking a bus to Miami. It took a lot of restraint to keep from busting out laughing."

"Very funny, wise guy. I hope you don't have any more surprises for me."

"Right now, I don't. But I'm sure I'll think of something." They both laughed.

At about ten fifteen, Mark received the call from Alex who gave him an estimate. Mark told him that it was fine and asked about what time they should pick up the car. Alex said it should be ready about five o'clock but that he would be there until six. After he hung up, Mark said, "Josh, I have to go to my room to make a phone call. Be right back."

In his room, Mark dialed the number thinking *Please be Aunt Sue, please be home.* After the fourth ring, the answering machine came on, "Please Leave a Message." Mark hung up. He didn't want to leave a message because what would he say? "Hello, I'm Mark and Josh is with me"? And suppose it's not Aunt Sue. No way. He decided to keep calling until a real person answered. He went back to the pool and told Josh. "No luck. I'll call back later."

At the pool it was obvious that Josh was enjoying himself especially when he was in the pool. Mark wondered how he learned how to swim. Josh loved the Jacuzzi and the sauna and Mark was elated that Josh was having so much fun. More progress. His only hope was that he had Aunt Sue's right number, and if so, that she comes through for Josh. Mark had called three times so far, ten thirty, eleven thirty, and one thirty.

Still no luck.

Then at two forty-five, Mark told Josh that he was going to try calling again. He went to the room, dialed the number and thought, *Please be home.* After the third ring, a voice at the other end said, "Hello."

Mark's heart skipped a beat and he said, "Hello, am I speaking to Sue Brennan?"

"Yes, may I ask who's calling?"

"My name is Mark. Do you happen to have a nephew named Josh?"

Sue shouted into the phone, "JOSH? YES, YES. Oh my god, did something happen to him? Is he all right? Where is he?"

"Mrs. Brennan, Josh is with me here in Key West, and physically he is fine, but emotionally he's not so fine."

Mark heard Aunt Sue crying as she asked, "Is he with you now? Can I talk to him?"

"He's down by the pool and he doesn't know I am calling you. I didn't tell him because I wasn't sure I had the right number."

"We haven't seen Josh in seven years. We had no idea where he was. We even hired a private detective and even he couldn't find him. Josh was like another son to John and me. We all loved him. When we couldn't find him, we all cried a lot including my two sons, Jared and Jason."

"Mrs. Brennan—"

She interrupted and said, "Please call me Sue."

"Thank you Sue. Josh told me a lot about you, his Uncle John and Jared and Jason. He told me how much you did for him and how much fun he had with you and your family. As he was telling me about you, he was crying. He still loves you very much."

Sue was still softly crying, "I've often wondered why Josh never tried to contact us. He knew where we lived and he had our phone number, unless he lost the number. Do you know why?"

"Sue, I think it's better that Josh tells you the story. But I will say the last six or seven years have been extremely difficult for him . . . and that's an understatement. As far as I know he was basically alone and on his own even though he lived with his parents."

"Oh my god, that poor boy."

"Here's the problem. He left home yesterday and for some reason he drove here to Key West. I only met him last night and I've trying to help him. The point is he has no place to go."

Sue screams into phone, "YES, HE DOES! He can live with us. I want him here."

"I was hoping, correction, I was praying you would say that. I am so relieved. But may I make a suggestion. This is a major decision for you and your family. Don't you think it would be better to discuss it with your family to see if they agree with you, especially the two boys?"

"Yes, I suppose you are right. Whenever we have a big decision to make we always gather as a group to discuss it. It's now close to 3:00 p.m. I'll call my husband and the boys and ask them to come home as quickly as possible, but I don't want to tell them why until they are home. Can I call you back?" Mark gave her his cell number and asked about what time she would be calling. Sue replied, "I'm sure they can all get here in about twenty or thirty minutes, so why don't we say about four."

"Perfect. Now when you call, Josh will be in the room with me and will not have known that I called you. When you tell me what you decided, I will be noncommittal so as to not let on what's being discussed. If your decision is positive, I'll put Josh on the phone."

"Thank you so much, Mark, for helping Josh and for calling me. I am so happy." Mark heard her crying again. "I'll call around four."

After they said their goodbyes, Mark headed for the pool to find Josh on an air inflatable raft in the pool. When Josh saw him, he got out and said, "Wow, I guess you got through. That was a long call. Guess it was important."

"It was Josh, that it was." Mark had a smile on his face as he said it.

During the next hour, Mark kept looking at his watch in anticipation. This did not go unnoticed by Josh who asked why he kept looking at his watch. Mark told him he was expecting an important call.

At three fifty, Mark said, "Come on. Let's go to my room and right after I get my call, we'll head out to get your car."

In the room, Mark told Josh to help himself to snacks and soda which he did. Josh said, "Mark, I had such a good time today. I don't remember the last time I had such a good time. Thank you." When his cell rang, Mark jumped up and quickly answered it.

"Hello."

"Mark, this is Sue. Is Josh with you?"

"Yes."

"We discussed it and we all want him here to be part of our family, and Jared and Jason are elated."

"I see."

"Mark, put him on the phone please."

"One moment please . . . Josh, it's for you."

Josh said with a puzzled look on his face, "Me? Who could be calling me?"

"Josh, there's only one way to find out. Take the phone."

"Uh, hello."

Sue almost shouted into the phone, "Josh, oh Josh, this is your Aunt Sue."

Josh stared at the phone with a questioning look on his face.

"Josh, Josh, are you there?"

"Aunt . . . Aunt Sue . . . is . . . is it . . . really . . . you?"

"Yes, honey baby."

"Oh my god, that's what you used to call me. It really is you!"

Josh dropped the phone on the bed and loudly started to cry as he put his hands to his face. Mark went to Josh, took the phone and said, "Sue, hold on for a few. He is overcome with emotion. Let me try to calm him down."

Mark put his arm around Josh's shoulder and said, "It's okay Josh, let it out." He started to rock Josh, his loud sobs slowly turning into whimpers.

"Are you all right, Josh?" Josh stopped crying and Mark said, "Are you ready to talk to Aunt Sue. She loves you so much and she's waiting for you."

Josh said, "I'm all right now." He took the phone and said, "I'm sorry, Aunt Sue. It's just that I was so happy to hear your voice. I'm fine now."

"It's okay, honey. I want you to know that I, I mean, we all love you. We tried for a long time to find you and we never forgot you."

"And I love all of you. I thought about you every day, hoping someday I'd see you again."

"Josh, honey, we all want you to come live with us. We talked about it and we want you to become part of our family."

"Really, Aunt Sue?"

"Yes, really. Josh, we're on speaker phone and all the boys want to say hello."

Uncle John spoke next, "Josh, this is Uncle John. How are you, kiddo?"

"Uncle John . . . oh Uncle John, I remember you always called me kiddo. I miss you so much."

"Josh, don't worry about a thing. All your worries are now behind you. You have a family now, a family that loves you."

Josh started to whimper again and said, "Uncle John, I . . . I want to believe that . . . but . . ."

"Believe it Josh . . . believe *in* it. We want you to live with us."

"Thank you, Uncle John."

"Hey Josh, this is Jared. How ya doin', cuz?"

"Oh wow . . . Jared. I can't believe this."

"Do you remember how much fun you, Jason and I used to have? Well, we're going to have even more fun when we see you. Seriously, dude, we want you here."

"Joshie, it's me, your favorite cousin, Jason."

"Oh, Jason. I remember you always called me Joshie and I hated it. But now I love it."

"Now listen here, I happen to be the ruler of this roost, so what I say goes. You *are* going to live with us and that's final. I need a better big brother than what I have now."

In the background, Josh heard Jared yelling, "Hey, watch it little bro." And for the first time, Josh laughed. Jason then said, "Please Josh, please say you will come and live with us . . . please."

Aunt Sue then spoke, "All right, all right, that's enough for now. Josh, will you come and live with us?"

Josh looked at Mark with a questioning look. Mark said in a loud voice, "*Yes, Yes.*"

Aunt Sue, worrying about the short delay said, "Josh?"

"Aunt Sue, there is nothing in this world that I would like better." Josh then heard loud cheers of approval.

"Wonderful, how soon can you come?"

"Hold on, let me talk to Mark. Mark, when do you think?"

"Josh, you can leave anytime you want . . . tomorrow, the day after, whenever."

"Well, I do want to spend some time with you. Today is Thursday, is it okay to stay two days and leave on Saturday?"

Mark replied, "Absolutely. Good idea."

"Aunt Sue, is Saturday okay?"

"Saturday is perfect. I'll give you our home phone number and address." She did and Josh repeated them for Mark to write down.

"Do you remember how to get to the house?"

"The same house? My parents told me you moved to California. But I do remember how to get there."

"So that's why you never called us. You poor boy. But that's behind us now, so why don't you call us on Saturday when you're ready to leave so we know about what time to expect you."

"I will, Aunt Sue."

"Good, we'll finally see you on Saturday, and please, drive carefully."

"I will, Aunt Sue, and thank you so much. I love all of you."

"And we love you."

They said their goodbyes and Josh looked at Mark, jumped up and hugged him. "Thank you Mark. I don't how you did it. You are so amazing and I am so happy."

Mark laughed and said, "Hey wait. What about Miami?"

"Funny, very funny. Would you tell me how you found them?"

"Sure, but first take another shower to wash all that chlorine off, and then we'll go get your car. I'll tell you on the way to the mechanic's station."

When they arrived at the station, Alex came out to greet them, "You're all set. It's almost like new. Listen to the engine. New carburetor, new alternator, new plugs and points, new tires. Everything else checked out fine. This baby will give you a lot of miles."

Mark said, "Thanks Alex, for getting it done on such short notice. This is a big load off my mind."

Josh chimed in, "Yeah, mine too. Thank you, sir."

Alex then gave Mark the bill. Mark tried to hide it from Josh but was too late. Josh saw it and blurted out, "Oh my god, almost fifteen hundred dollars!"

Mark said, "No problem, my man."

On the way back to the hotel, Josh was still in disbelief at all that was happening to him and he kept thanking Mark. He said, "Mark, this car runs just great. I can't believe it. I don't know how I can repay you but I *am* going to try."

Mark replied, "Josh, I already told you how you can repay me. Just remember your sacred vow. How about we go out to a nice restaurant to celebrate your upcoming reunion with your new family. I know of a nice French restaurant. They have the best *Duck L'Orange*."

"You expect me to eat a duck?"

"Yup, and escargot."

"What's that?"

"Snails in their shell prepared with butter and garlic."

"Ducks and snails . . . ugh."

Mark laughed.

All the way back from the restaurant to the hotel, Josh kept repeating how much he loved the duck and escargot. And he loved the *crème brûlée*. He said it was the best meal he ever had and that he couldn't wait to tell Aunt Sue about it.

When they arrived at the hotel it was close to 9:00 p.m. Mark asked, "Do you want to do something or just hang around and relax."

"I *am* kinda beat. It's been the best day of my life. I'd rather just hang around. Uh, I'd like to ask you something and I hope you don't get mad at me."

"I won't get mad."

"If it's a bad idea, just tell me. But do you think . . . uh . . . uh . . . well, do you think you can hold me for a while. I think I just need to be hugged for a little."

For the next thirty minutes or so, they sat on Mark's bed, no talking, just 'friends' supporting each other. Josh then said, "Thanks Mark, I feel a lot better. I'm going to my room. I'll probably fall asleep in about 5.3 seconds."

Friday would be Josh's last day in Key West . . . and with his friend Mark. At breakfast, Mark asked Josh what he wanted to do today. Josh asked Mark to decide. So Mark thought a little and said, "How about we do some water stuff like scuba diving, water skiing, jet skiing, stuff like that."

"Huh? I've never done stuff like that. I wouldn't know how. Heck, I'm lucky I know how to swim . . . barely."

"Well it's about time you learned. I'll show you how to water ski and jet ski. It'll be fun."

So that's how they spent the day. Josh had a great time. After his sixth or seventh try, he was finally able to stand up on his skis. When he did stand for the first time, he started yelling and screaming in joy. Josh was even more thrilled with the snorkeling and especially with the jet skis. Mark encouraged him all the way. He was so happy that Josh was so happy. More than once during the day, Mark thought, *I'm really going to miss him.*

On the way back to the hotel, Josh couldn't contain his joy and enthusiasm.

"I had the greatest time today. I thought I'd never be able to stand up on the skis. I took some big floppers before I got the hang of it. The snorkeling was fantastic. Jet skiing is so exciting. The best day of my life."

Josh went on and on during the thirty-minute drive back to the hotel. Mark just sat alongside with a big smile on his face, enjoying Josh's enthusiastic 'performance'.

For dinner, Mark took Josh to a seafood restaurant.

"Seafood? I never had that before. In fact, I don't think I ever had any kind of fish."

"Well it's about time you did."

Mark ordered dinner that started with lobster bisque which was followed by a seafood sampler appetizer. On the huge platter were jumbo shrimp, oysters on the half shell, squid and scallops. For the entrée, Mark chose the crab-stuffed lobster tails.

Josh enjoyed the bisque, but when the sampler was put on the table his eyes bulged. He said, "The shrimp I recognize although I've never ate them, but what are the rest?"

Mark told him what each was and Josh cried out, "*Look*! I think they forgot to cook the oysters. They look raw." Mark laughed and said they are supposed to be raw.

Josh scrunched his face and asked, "What is squid? They look all wrinkly." Mark laughed again and said it's octopus. Josh looked at the plate, then at Mark, then at the plate again. He scrunched again and said, "Come on Mark, do you really expect me to eat raw oysters and octopus?"

To which Mark said, "Yup."

Very cautiously and with much, *much* apprehension, Josh sampled each item. And with each one, he said either "Wow," "Great," "Fantastic," "Hmmm," and other exclamations of delight. And when it came to the crab-stuffed lobster, he thought he was in seventh heaven. He ate so much that he turned down dessert. As they left the restaurant Josh proclaimed, "That meal was the best I ever had. I even loved the raw oysters and octopus."

On the way back to the hotel, Josh suddenly became very quiet and Mark thought it was because he ate so much. At the hotel they decided to sit by the pool and Mark now knew something was wrong.

"Okay, Josh, out with it. What's wrong?"

"Oh nothing," pause "except now I feel kinda sad."

To which Mark asked why.

"Well, I'm leaving tomorrow."

"And that makes you sad?"

"It's not that." Mark saw the tears fall from his eyes. "It's that I'll be leaving you, and I may never see you again."

"We can always keep in touch . . . phone, email, texting. Just remember that if you ever need anything or if you need help or you just want to talk, I'm just a phone call away. I'll always, and I mean always, be there for you."

"I know that, Mark. Do you think you can come to see me sometime?"

"We can work that out. First, get settled in with your new family. I know for a fact that you are going to be very happy. By the way, there is something that we never talked about."

"What's that?"

"School. I never asked you about it. Do you go to school?"

"Oh yeah, I graduated high school last month. You know, I never missed a day of school. I suppose the reason was that I wanted out of that house as much as possible to avoid the drinking, the drugs, the partying and the arguing. I hated them and that house so much."

"How did you do in school?

"All right I guess, some Bs, some Cs."

"Do you plan on going to college?"

"I never even thought about that."

"Okay, promise time. Promise me that you will talk to your aunt and uncle about college. I'm sure there's a community college in your area."

"Gee, I would like to go to college. Yeah, I will definitely talk to Aunt Sue and Uncle John about it."

"Great. How about your friends?"

"No friends, Mark. Never had time."

"You look tired, Josh."

"Yeah, from all that food, and probably thinking about tomorrow."

"What time do you think you'll want to leave?"

"Well, it *is* a long drive, probably three or four hours so I was thinking about nine."

"Do you want to meet in the cafe about 8?"

"That sounds good."

"When you get to your room, call the front desk and ask for a wake-up call."

"Will do." They both got up and hugged each other for a good long time.

Josh went to his room, but Mark headed for the ATM.

The next morning, Josh walked into the cafe looking very tired and serious. As he sat at Mark's table, Mark said, "I guess you didn't sleep too well last night."

"Yeah, I'm just nervous about today, happy in one way, but sad in another."

After they ordered breakfast, Mark said, "I was thinking about your car. It never occurred to me until last night. I kinda had a restless night also, and I thought about all the things you said to me. When you got, or forced," smile on Mark face, "your father to sign over the car, I guess you just wanted to get out of there as soon as possible."

"You got that right."

"So I'm assuming that you didn't have time to go to the Motor Vehicle Agency to register the car."

"Oh my god, I never even thought about that. What should I do?"

"There nothing you can do here, so I would suggest when you're driving back, make sure you stay *below* the speed limit. But don't drive ultra-slowly because that could attract attention. When you leave here, shake off your nerves and anxiety and focus on the task ahead . . . driving carefully. When you get there, tell your Aunt Sue and Uncle John that you need to register the car. Do you have a driver's license?"

"That I do have, and I'll be careful. Any other suggestions?"

After the waiter set down their breakfast, Mark continued, "Yes, one major one. After you're settled into your room, ask your aunt and uncle if you can talk to them."

"About what?"

"Josh, I think you should tell them the whole story of all you went through all these years . . . everything."

"Everything? But I don't want anyone to feel sorry for me."

"Yes, everything. You told me some of the things and as you spoke, yes, I did feel sorry for what you went through. But when you were done, I no longer felt sympathy, I felt admiration for you. When you tell your story to your aunt, uncle and two cousins, they will react the same way I did. They will feel sorry as you tell them, but when you finish, within couple of minutes, their sympathy or pity will end and they will look forward to your future with optimism as so should you."

Mark continued, "The main reason I think you should tell them is because I think it would be therapeutic. I mean, I think it would be good therapy for you. Once you're done, you can throw away the story as if it's no longer part of your past. You're no longer with your parents, you no longer fear them and you no longer have to think about them. I really believe it will take a big burden off your shoulders."

"That makes a lot of sense. You're absolutely right . . . you're always right. Now I do want to tell them about my past, and I will. Thanks again, Mark."

"Before we go, I have something to give to you." He handed Josh an envelope. Josh asked what is was and Mark said, "Just something to help you along the way."

Josh opened the envelope and his eyes bulged out as he saw a thick wad of money.

"I can't take this after all the money you spent on me! No way. Here, take it back."

"Mark, I want you to have it. Please do me this one favor. You're going to need to buy a lot of things when you get home. Besides, if you're serious in wanting us to keep in touch, then my condition is that you take this. Please, Josh, it would mean a lot to me."

More tears from Josh, "Oh my god, how . . . much . . . is . . . it?"

"You really want to know?" Josh nodded. "Okay, I'll tell you. It's only $800."

"Oh my god. That's way too much."

"Good, now that it's settled, we'd better head out. But first, here are my home phone number and email address. Let's go."

When they got to the car, they briefly stood there looking at each other. Then Josh hugged Mark and cried. He said, "Mark, I'm going to miss you. I love you so much."

"I'm going to miss you, and I love you as well." For the first time since he met Josh, tears started to fall from Mark's eyes. Trying to stay strong, he said, "I have an idea. We can always Skype with each other. This way we can talk and see one another." Tears were still flowing from both of them.

Josh said, "Yeah, great idea. Mark, can you do me a favor and email me your memoir. I want to read the whole thing. I'll have to send you my email address and phone number and stuff, and don't forget, I want you to come and visit me."

"Sure, I'll send it and I will visit if you want me to. Josh, after you get settled in at your new home, could you give me a call so that I know you arrived safely?" Josh said he would do that.

"Mark, thank you for all you've done for me and thank you for saving my life."

"How about one last hug." After one last and long hug, Mark said, "Okay, get going and drive safely. Bye for now."

"I will, I promise. Bye for now Mark." Josh drove off to his new family.

Josh arrived in Browning in good time, only three and one half hours. It was now 12:20 p.m. When he saw a convenience store, he was sure of the way to Aunt Sue's and Uncle John's house. He got on their street about ten minutes later and slowly and nervously drove toward the house. When he got there, he parked in front of the house and was shocked when he saw a huge banner hanging on the house. The banner read "WELCOME HOME, JOSH." He grabbed his backpack and slowly got out of the car, never taking his eyes off the banner. He stopped and just stood there staring at it with tears in his eyes.

Then the front door opened, and Aunt Sue came running down the walkway yelling, "JOSH, JOSH!"

When she got to him, she hugged him tightly and Josh hugged her just as tightly. Aunt Sue said through her tears, "Oh, Josh honey, you don't know how happy I am to see you. We've missed you so much."

Josh replied through his own tears, "Aunt Sue . . . Aunt Sue . . . I thought I'd never see you again. You're more beautiful than ever. I love you so much."

As they continued hugging and crying, Uncle John, Jared and Jason were standing on the side giving Sue this private moment. Meanwhile, an individual was taping the whole thing.

Aunt Sue said, "And you know how much I love you too. I've always loved you. I always thought of you as my son. You're home at last."

"Thank you so much Aunt Sue."

Breaking the hug, Aunt Sue said, "Oh my, the boys are waiting to greet you."

Uncle John said to Jared and Jason, "Go on boys."

Jared replied, "No, dad, your turn, we want to go last."

So Uncle John went to Josh and gave him a big hug, lifting him in the air, turning in circles. "Welcome home Josh. We've been waiting for this day for years. You are now part of our family. We all love you."

With that, Josh's waterworks erupted anew as he cried on Uncle John shoulder. "There now, you are safe and you are home."

"Uncle John, I missed you so much. Thank you." Uncle John broke his hug and made a motion to Jared and Jason, nodding that they should come to Josh.

Jared said to Jason, "You take high and I'll take low." Jason nodded and both boys made a dash toward Josh with Jared tackling him and Jason jumping on his back. All three went sprawling to the ground. Aunt Sue began yelling, "Jared, Jason . . . what are you doing? Stop it right now." As she started to go to them Uncle John stopped her and held her by her arm. The boys were still wrestling. "Jared, Jason, stop this."

Jason popped his head up and faced his mother, "Chill out mom, we're just doing what the three of us used to do six years ago . . . and we always won."

Josh popped *his* head up, looked to his aunt and said, "Yeah, but that's because I used to let them win."

More wrestling. After several seconds or so, the wrestling match ended and the boys got up and dusted themselves off.

Josh said, "Wow, that was the best welcome ever. Thanks. But I bet you don't remember what we did after the wrestling match." With that, both Jared and Jason yelled, "GROUP HUG!" And the three boys got into their traditional group hug.

Sue asked John, "Did you know they used to do that?"

John replied, "Sure did."

"Did you put the boys up to this today?"

"No, that was their doing."

Josh said, "I can't believe that banner. It is so cool."

Jared replied, "It was Jason's idea and both of us made the banner and Dad helped us put it up."

Jason said, "Didn't we do a great job?"

Josh replied, "You sure did. Thank you. I was nervous when I pulled up to your house but when I saw that banner, I was so relieved. You guys are the best. Wait a minute. I'm not sure, but Jared, I think you're fifteen now, and Jason, you must be thirteen. Is that right?"

"You got it right, cuz."

Aunt Sue then said, "All right, let's all go inside and get Josh settled in."

When they were inside, Josh looked around and said, "Wow, this is like a mansion. It's more beautiful than I remember."

Jared said, "Wait till you see the rest of it. Come on, we want to show our back yard."

Both Jared and Jason took one of Josh's hand and hurried to the yard. Jason said, "Look, isn't it cool?"

Josh said, "Yeah, cool and fantastic. Wow! Look at the size of that pool, and a Jacuzzi and a net. Is that for volleyball or something?"

"That's enough, boys. Show Josh to his room and let him get settled in. Josh, dear, are you hungry? I can fix you a nice lunch."

"No thanks, Aunt Sue, I stopped off for a Whopper on the way here."

Before they went upstairs, Josh said to Aunt Sue and Uncle John, "If it's okay, I'd like to talk to you when I'm done. I'd like to tell you about these past ten years."

Aunt Sue said, "Are you sure, honey?"

Uncle John added, "You don't have to Josh. We won't expect you to."

"Aunt Sue, Uncle John, I want to tell you, and I need to tell you about it all."

"Okay, honey, whenever you want."

So the two boys, followed by Josh, noisily ran upstairs and brought Josh to his room. "Whoa, is this my room? I hope I'm not putting you guys out or anything."

Jared said, "Yeah, it's all yours, and Jason and I have our own room."

Jason joined in and said, "Empty your backpack and we'll go back downstairs. We want to show you our game room."

Josh did that and Jared said, "Is that all you have?"

"Yup, that's everything."

Jared said, "We have to do something about that."

Josh then said, "You know, I can't believe how much you two have grown. I almost didn't recognize you. The last time I saw you two, you were just little pipsqueaks."

"Pipsqueaks!" both boys shouted.

Josh laughed and said, "Yeah, and now you're big pipsqueaks."

"Let's get him," Jason yelled and both boys rushed Josh and tackled him to the bed.

Jared then said, "That's enough for now. The 'rents are waiting. Come on, let's go."

Josh said, "But first I have to make a phone call. I have to call Mark to tell him I made it all right. Is there a phone I can use? I didn't register mine yet."

Jared said, "Here, use mine."

Josh called and when Mark picked up, Josh said, "Mark, I'm here. I made it all right. Yes, everything is fine. When I got here, there was a big banner hanging on the house. It read, 'Welcome Home, Josh.' Yeah, Jared and Jason made it. Yes, Mark. I am so happy. Yes.

I going down now to talk to my aunt and uncle. I will. I'll call you again when things are more settled and I'll write more details in an email. Yes, and thank you so much. I love you, Mark. Bye."

They went to the game room in the basement level and Josh stood there in shock. He saw a pool table, a ping-pong table, exercise equipment and video games. "Whoa, this is unbelievable!"

Jason said, "Yeah, and I'm the video king, but Jared is the ping pong and pool king. But someday I'll catch up and whup him."

Jared asked, "Do you want to play something now?"

"Thanks, Jared, but I have to talk to your parents."

"About what?"

"I guess where I've been since I saw you last and all that went on."

"Uh, could we come? We'd like to hear about it."

"Jared, I really would like you and Jason to be there."

When they got upstairs, they found Aunt Sue in the kitchen. "Aunt Sue, the room is beautiful. Thank you."

"Before we go inside, let me take a good look at you without teary eyes. Oh my, you are such a handsome young man."

Josh blushed, but Jason proudly said, "Yeah, he takes after me." They all laughed.

Aunt Sue said, "You're all handsome young men."

Jason and Jared beamed while Josh blushed again.

"Now Josh, I think you have time for a small snack." She put a covered plate on the table, then unveiled the plate and Josh, wide-eyed, was staring at a plate full of golden brown chocolate chip cookies."

"Oh my god," he cried out. "I don't believe I am seeing this. I always loved your chocolate chip cookies. Aunt Sue, you didn't forget. Wow!"

"I remember how much you loved them. Try one and tell me what you think."

With a big smile, Josh took a bite from one of the cookies, slowly chewed and closed his eyes as he savored his favorite snack. "Oh, Aunt Sue, I think I'm in heaven. They are so good, better than I remembered. Oh wow."

As Aunt Sue set three glasses of milk on the table she said, "Now you three have your cookies and milk while I go inside to see what's needed. And Jason, no more than twenty this time."

"Aw Mom, can I help it if they are so good? Josh, they're my favorite too."

"Yeah, me too. But you better start eating before Jason gobbles them all up."

"Aw, Jared."

Five minutes or so later, Aunt Sue returned and asked, "Are you boys all done?"

"Yes Aunt Sue, thank you."

"Then let's go inside and get comfortable."

Jared added, "Mom, Josh said it was all right for us to be there."

"By all means, dear, come."

In the living room, Uncle John was sitting there chatting with two men. When the boys and Aunt Sue walked in, Uncle John stood up and approached Josh. "Josh, I want you to meet some friends." They walked over to the two men.

"This is William Stafford. Bill, this is our beloved nephew, Josh." They shook hands.

"I'm very happy to meet you Josh. I've heard a lot about you. Don't worry, all good stuff." Josh got good vibes from Mr. Stafford and thought he would like him.

"It's nice meeting you, Mr. Stafford."

"Josh, this is his associate, Daniel Conway." They shook hands.

"Josh, it is so good meeting you, and I heard about the good stuff too. By the way, I was the guy behind the camera outside."

Josh smiled and once again felt the vibes. "Nice meeting you too, Mr. Conway."

They all sat down and Uncle John said, "Josh, Bill and Daniel are our close friends and they also are our lawyers. I hope you don't mind, but I asked them to come in case there are legal issues we need to know about."

Bill Stafford explained, "Josh, we are here on your behalf to make sure you are protected. But on the other hand, since this is a family matter between you and your aunt, uncle and cousins, you may want to discuss this privately. Then if there are legal questions, your Uncle John can call us and we can deal with them. So we don't absolutely need to be here. Either way, if you want us to be, we would be your lawyer. As such, we are bound by lawyer-client confidentiality which means legally we are prohibited from revealing anything you say to us."

"I understand, Mr. Stafford, and I do want you and Mr. Conway to stay. And if I need a lawyer, I want you two."

Then with a slight smile Josh said, "Besides, if you're good enough for my aunt and uncle, you're good enough for me." Chuckles from everyone.

Daniel Conway then said, "Thank you, Josh. We were told that you may want to tell your aunt, uncle and cousins about your life while living in your parents' home. Is that your intention today?"

"Yes, sir."

"Then Bill and I have a suggestion to make for your own protection and/or for possible future use if litigation would become necessary. We strongly recommend that you allow us to video tape what you are about to say. It is also covered under lawyer-client confidentiality, and no one will ever see it unless you authorize it."

"I don't mind, sir."

"Good. Now, let me set things up for the camera angle." Daniel had Sue and John sit on the sofa with Josh between them. He then moved two chairs for Jared and Jason, angling them so that both their faces would be seen through the camera. He put the camera on the tripod, checked the focus and lighting, then said, "All set."

After a few instructions, Josh was told to take his time and begin whenever he was ready. Josh sat on the sofa, leaned back and closed his eyes. About thirty seconds later, he opened his eyes and began. "Aunt Sue, Uncle John, before I start I have to tell why I want to do this. When I was Key West, Mark helped me a lot and I'll tell you about him later. He also gave me good advice. He's a really smart guy and he used to be a high school teacher. This morning before I left to come here, he suggested that I tell you my story so to speak. I asked why and he said that he thought it would be therapeutic for me. That once I tell my new family about these past years, it would take a big weight off my shoulders. And that after I did this, I could rid myself of my past, like I'd be throwing it away. And I would never even think about my parents again. The way he explained it made sense to me. The night before, I told Mark a little about what I went through and I did feel a little better."

"So to get on with it, ever since I met you when I was six years old, I always considered you to be my parents. My biological parents never loved or liked me. I was an inconvenience to them. They only kept me around to use me by making me clean up the house, like scrubbing floors, washing dishes and all the other work that needed to be done in and around the house. The only time they ever talked to me was to order me to do something. The only food they gave me was cold cuts for sandwiches. But there were many, many days when I went without food."

"I don't remember them ever calling me by my name. They would call me a 'worthless piece of crap' or 'useless' or 'you little s—t,' and worse names like 's———d,' 'b———d,' 'f——g idiot,' and other names." Josh did not say the words. "I didn't know what some of those words meant but they made me feel really bad."

Aunt Sue then hugged Josh more tightly. Uncle John, William Stafford and Daniel Conway all stared at Josh with serious expressions. Jared and Jason also stared with wide eyes and open mouths. Josh, to his credit, did not shed one tear.

"But the worse part was the noise. Almost every night, they would have friends over having a party, drinking a lot . . . beer . . . whiskey . . . and doing drugs. And there was a terrible smell in the house that I later found out was marijuana. I couldn't sleep until their partying stopped. I was tired and hungry all the time, and I was just plain sad. Practically every night, I cried myself to sleep."

"I'll tell you what got me through all this. The reason I had hope, and the reason I was able to survive."

Josh took out his most precious possession. He showed the picture to his aunt, uncle, two cousins and the two lawyers. It was a picture of the Brennan family with Josh in the middle. "That first night in the new house, I took the picture out and spoke to you. I remember I was crying and I said, 'I know you didn't leave me.' Well, every single night, without fail, I took the picture out and talked to you, usually for a couple of minutes. It was like I was having a conversation with you, and I'd make believe you were talking to me. I did this every night for seven years. Sounds crazy, but Aunt Sue, Uncle John, Jared, Jason, you are the only reason I survived." Josh was loudly crying as he said this, and did Aunt Sue, Jared and Josh were also softly crying. Uncle John and the two lawyers were teary-eyed. When Josh regained his composure he said, "I know you're all probably wondering why I didn't tell anybody. Well, I was scared of them. They kept telling me that if I told anyone about them, they would hurt me really bad or kill me and all of you. I was so scared."

"The first time I saw you Aunt Sue, you hugged me and I was never hugged by anyone before. At that moment, I felt safe in your arms. Then you started taking me to your house, and when I first met Uncle John and Jared and Jason, I saw what a real family was and I wanted so much to be part of it. I remember the first time I had dinner at your house the day after we met. I'll never forget it. We had salad, spaghetti and meat balls and garlic bread. That was the first time I ever had a cooked meal. I loved it." Josh paused, took a couple of deep breaths, then continued.

"You started to do a lot of things for me, taking me places like the park and the pool. You even bought me clothes and other stuff kids need. Being with you, I was happy for the first time in my life . . . until I had to go home. Then I was miserable again. When my parents saw all this, they started saying mean things about all of you. They told me that they hated you. They told me if I ever said anything to any of you about them they would kill me and all of you. I promised him over and over that I wouldn't. That's why I never said anything to you. My parents resented that I was spending so much time with you. Then he stopped letting you in the house. Every night, he locked me in my room, and when I thought I could get away with it, I sneaked out through the window in my room and went to your house. I remember the times when my father told you to keep away from me, you just ignored him."

"When I was about seven years old, things just got worse. One day, when you bought me new sneakers, my father saw them and started to yell and curse at me. For the first time, he slapped me in the face. I ran to my room and cried. He would do that whenever he was in the mood which was just about every day. He would punch me real hard in the arm or stomach or kick me and that really hurt. That's when I started wearing long-sleeved shirts—to hide the bruises. I tried my best to avoid him especially when he was drunk. My mother was just bad. She would hit me for any reason, like if she didn't like how I cleaned the house. Many times to punish me, they wouldn't let me eat anything."

"Then when my father punched me in the face and gave me that black eye, I tried to hide it all day. But then you saw me. I remember how mad you were, and you took me to your house and took care of my eye. The very next day, the police showed up and questioned my parents. They told the officers it was an accident. When the police asked me what happened, I told them I wasn't sure. I was still scared that they would do something bad to me or you. The police gave them some kind of citation and said they were going to report the incident to their superiors."

"The same day, someone from the Child Protective Service showed up. She talked to me alone and I didn't know what to say. Basically, I told her the same thing I told the police. She talked to my parents and told them that she would be writing a report and would talk to her superiors. I'm not sure, but I think she said they would probably be taking custody. I really didn't know what she meant."

"Later that day, I heard my father on the phone yelling and screaming that he needed the papers today. He said he would pay ten thousand dollars. At that time, I had no idea what he was talking about. The very next morning, I was in my bedroom and my father came in and told me to throw all my things in paper bags because we were moving. I asked him where we were moving to and he slapped me in the face and said, 'Shut up, you worthless piece of scum. From now on things are going to be different.' Then I asked if you knew we were moving, and he punched me in the face so hard that I fell back and landed on the floor. He said, 'Your precious aunt and uncle moved to California so you'll never see them again. And I don't ever want to hear their names ever again.' I ran to my room and cried. But I was thinking to myself, 'Aunt Sue and Uncle John would never leave me.'"

"At the new house, the first thing my father said to me was that we had to change my name. I asked why and he told me to shut my mouth and listen. My new name was Greg Smith. He told me that if I ever told anyone about my old name, I would wish I was never born. I think he was reading my mind because I was wishing just that."

"That night, I walked into the living room where my parents were drinking as usual and my father yelled, 'What the hell do you want?' I said I was hungry and there was no food. He said, 'Too bad. Now get lost.' Since that day, it was a question of survival, not knowing if and when I would have food to eat. Sometimes there would be a little food in the house, but there were many, many times when there was none. I was hungry all the time." As Josh was talking, Aunt Sue, Jared and Jason were silently crying. Tears were flowing from Uncle John's eyes.

"One day, I was walking around and saw a food place with tables and chairs outside. So I stood there and watched people eating. I noticed that one person didn't eat everything and he left unfinished food on the table. So trying not to be noticed, I went to the table and sat down. I looked around and saw that no one was looking at me, so I ate the scraps. I went there many times, but most times no one left anything on the tables. So I . . . I would—" Josh began to cry heavily, "I searched through the garbage cans for food. From that day on, I searched garbage cans many times, but most of the time there was nothing and what I was able to find was not too much."

Josh paused and wiped his eyes and continued, "This went on for a long time and the beatings continued, so I started to leave the house early every day just to avoid being hit. I'd just walk around and come back late. I hated my drunken parents, and I hated being in that house. The loud, drunken parties continued at the house and it got even worse."

"I turned twelve years old and since it was late August, my mother took me to a school to register me. She pulled out my old school records and my birth certificate. Since I was sitting next to her, I could plainly see the name Greg Smith on the birth certificate and I also saw the name Greg Smith on the school records. It all clicked then and there. Even at twelve years old, I knew that they had forged the birth certificate and altered the school records. The guidance counselor had no clue."

Aunt Sue said, "Oh my god, that explains it. That's why we couldn't find you. Honey, we spent nearly a year looking for you. We even hired a private detective, and he couldn't find you either."

Josh, with more tears in his eyes, then gave Aunt Sue a hug and said, "Thank you for trying."

"About a week before school started, on one of my walks I noticed at a nearby house a man in his yard, on his knees pulling weeds. I was thinking maybe the man would let me help and maybe he'd give me some food. So I asked him if he needed help. To my surprise, he said he sure did and that it would take him forever. I got down on my knees and started to pull weeds. The man said I needed gloves so he went inside. A couple minutes later, he came out with gloves and two glasses of lemonade and some cookies. Boy, I devoured those cookies. I saw the man stretching and rubbing his back so I said to him, 'If your back is sore, I can finish.' He said, 'You don't mind?' 'No, I'll be happy to.'"

"I think it took about an hour but I got it all done. The man thanked me and handed me fifteen dollars. I thanked him and said it was too much but he insisted. I asked him if he had any other work for me to do. He said not now but maybe in about a week. I asked him if anyone else in the neighborhood needed help and I told him I could use the money. He asked for what. Without thinking, I said for food. As soon as I said it, I regretted it. He asked about my parents. I lied and told him they were very sick and I needed to help them out. He asked if I had a phone and I said no, so he said to stop by in a couple of days and he'd see what he can do."

"I walked away happy as can be, wondering what I should do with the money. I decided to hold onto it and use it on food, but only when I absolutely had to. I took the fifteen dollars out of my pocket, took my shoe off and put the money in my socks, knowing that if my parents ever saw it they would take it. So the man did have another job for me, cleaning out his garage. He also hooked me up with another neighbor who needed work done in his yard."

"Things were looking up, and within a month I had $30. I knew I needed some clothes and sneakers. I thought I could get money from my parents, but only after begging and getting beat up. No way. I'd go to Goodwill or the Salvation Army for what I need. I got all I needed for free."

"School began and I was entering the seventh grade. I did like the new school, and one of the classes was Physical Education. We did calisthenics a lot, and I enjoyed that. I liked the teacher, he was a really nice guy. One day I went into his office after school and asked him if I could talk to him. He told me to have a seat. I asked him if there was a way I could get stronger, like build up my arms and legs. He asked me why. I said so I could protect myself against bullies. He asked me if I had been bullied in school. I said not this school. I lied and said it was at my previous school."

"He asked how old I was, and I replied twelve. He said I was too young for weights. Instead, he gave me an exercise program that included push-ups, sit-ups, pull-ups, running, and a couple other things. He gave me the information, took my weight and told me he'd check on my development from time to time. Every single day, I did each exercises and ran at least two miles, sometimes more."

"When I was going to school, I would get to school early, usually about 7:00 a.m. to do some homework. During lunch periods I went to the school library. I would also go the town library some nights and on weekends. There was no way I could do any studying at that house with all their partying and arguing. I would do anything or go any place to stay out of that house until I thought it was safe. I never missed a day of school because it was like a safe haven for me. But food was a major problem. Sometimes when I sneaked into the house, there were cold cuts. So I would eat while my parents and their friends were drinking and doing drugs. Most times there was nothing there to eat. If my father heard me come in, he would come to me, very drunk, and hit me for no reason, asking me where I've been."

"And that's how it went for the whole year while I was in the seventh grade, always worrying about when I would eat again since my $30 was gone. I used it for food the times when I went two or three days without food. "

"When I was in the eighth grade, I still saw my PE Teacher who checked on my development. He felt the muscles on my arms and legs and said, 'Wow!' He then told me to lift up a barbell, then another bigger one. There was a big stuffed canvas bag and he told me that when you punched it, it would make an impression and that would give him an indication of my strength. So I punched it hard with each hand. He looked at the impression and said 'Wow' again. He said, 'I feel sorry for the guy who messes with you.' Then he started giving me pointers about how to fight and where to land a punch, and then defense moves."

"I was ready."

"I was thirteen years old by then, a couple months before I became fourteen. I was pretty big for my age, standing about five feet, eight inches. As I walked out of school, I kept thinking of all the beatings I received and I got madder and madder."

"For the first time in a long time, I went straight home. I usually went into the house quietly through the back door, but this time I walked in the front door and deliberately slammed the door hard. My father looked at me and asked what did I think I was doing. He said if I ever slammed the door again he would kick the living s—t out of me. I went to the door, opened it, and slammed even harder than before. He came to me with clenched fists and took a swing but I easily sidestepped it. He turned to me and I let loose. I punched him first in the stomach and while he was doubled over, I punched him in his face. Down he went. I yelled, 'You want more? Get up!'"

Jason couldn't contain himself as he shouted, "Way to go, Josh!"

"My father was holding his eye and stayed down. 'Now you will see what it feels like to have a black eye.' I turned to my mother and said, 'Now you, lady, get your butt over here and sit down.' Whoa, did she move in a hurry."

"I hollered, 'Your days of hitting me are over. From now on leave me alone and I'll leave you alone. Do you understand me?' Finally, my father said, 'Yeah, yeah, we'll leave you alone. Just keep out of our way.' I said, 'With pleasure.'

"We never spoke to each other again. Sure, the loud and wild parties continued and I still had trouble sleeping with all the noise, but I figured there was nothing I could do about that. I didn't want to be confronted by all those guys. There must have been ten or twelve who were regular visitors."

"For the next two and a half years, I was still totally on my own, fending for myself, always thinking of scrounging for my next meal. I was still searching through garbage cans a lot. Once in a while, I would find some work with people in the area doing yard work, clean-up work or any such jobs. When there was food at the house, I would eat whatever was there, but most times there was nothing. So I had to use some of the money I earned to buy food. When I had some money, I bought jars of peanut butter and bread and some-times as a treat, jam for PB&J sandwiches. Peanut butter and bread was the only thing I bought because it wasn't expensive and it's very filling . . . and I could leave them in my room. I don't think I'll ever eat peanut butter again."

"During this time, I was dreaming of saving up for a laptop computer and a cell phone even though I knew it would take me a long time to save enough money. I asked my computer teacher how much I would need for both and he said probably about $800 which was a small fortune to me. But when I turned sixteen, I got a part-time job flipping burgers at McDonald's. I also got free food when I was working. So I began saving money."

"Finally my senior year came and I wanted so much to graduate and get out of that house. I took a Driver's Education course the summer before my senior year. But to do that, I had to get parent permission. So I got the forms, took them home and put them in front of my mother and sternly told her, 'Here, sign this.' She looked at me through her blood shot eyes, looked at the form and signed it. She didn't say a word. I think she was afraid of me."

"When I became eligible to take the driver's test for a license, the instructor gave me the forms. I went to the neighbor who first gave me work around his house. His name was Mr. Silban. I asked him if he would please take me for a driver's test. He agreed and I passed."

"After I graduated, I knew I was finally leaving that house so I bought a laptop and a cell phone. That left me with only about $50. So I worked for a couple of weeks and when I had $250, I quit my job."

"I picked a time when I knew my parents would be crashed out from their alcohol and drugs to search the house. I sneaked into their bedroom while they were sleeping and searched for what I was looking for. I saw a bunch of papers in a box, took it and quietly walked out and searched. There I found the title to my mother's car, put it aside and looked through the box again. I found the forged birth certificate and right behind it, I found my real birth certificate. I thought they were pretty dumb keeping it. I took all three papers."

"I went to the bedroom to return the box and put it in the closet where I found it. I then noticed a blanket covering something. It was a box about two feet high, three feet wide and one foot deep. I lifted the blanket and saw stacks of one hundred dollar bills wrapped in packs of $1,000 each. I tried to get a count but I stopped at $18,000 and I was less than halfway through. Then I saw cellophane-wrapped packages of drugs. Half were obviously marijuana and the other half probably cocaine. I thought I hit the jackpot. I said 'Gotcha'. I left everything as it was and left the room."

"When the day arrived when I was leaving, I threw everything I needed in my backpack. On the way out I grabbed my mother's car keys which were on table in the hall. I found my parents in the kitchen, I guess trying to get over their hangover with coffee. I took out the title to the car which was in my father's name, showed it to him and ordered him to sign the car over to me."

"Well, he erupted with many profanities and ended by yelling, 'There is no way in hell I'll sign this over to you. Who the hell do you think you are? Now get the hell out of here.'"

"I calmly took out my cell phone which wasn't in use since I didn't sign up with a phone company, but I knew they wouldn't know that. I punched 911. I said, 'Yes you will sign it over. You see this, it's 911. If you don't sign it over right now, I will call this number and tell the cops about all the drugs and stacks of money in your closet. This place with be swarming with police in minutes.'"

"My father was in total shock. He tried to say something but nothing came out of his mouth. 'Well, what's it going to be old man? Do I press this send button or do you sign? Listen, you sign this over and I promise I will not call the cops and you will never see me again.'"

My father looked at my mother who looked petrified. He then looked back at me, saw that my finger was on the send button and he finally said, 'How can I be sure you that you won't call the cops if I sign it over?'"

"You have my word for it. I don't want to call because if I do, I'd have to stay in this godforsaken place to give testimony. And I have no desire to do either. All I want to do is get out of this town as far away as possible and never see you again."

"My mother said, 'Victor, sign the damn thing. At least we'll be rid of the brat. That car is shot anyway.' He did and I was gone."

"I got on the highway and drove. Where to? I had no idea. But I do remember saying out loud, 'I did it Aunt Sue, Uncle John, Jared, Jason. I did it!' When I left the house I never thought about registering the car or insurance. Mark asked me about it. He told me to drive here ultra-carefully and to tell you when I got here. I do have a driver's license, though."

Uncle John said, "Don't worry about it. We'll take care of all that on Monday."

"Thank you, Uncle John. Well, I ended up in Key West and when I got there my car broke down. I pulled into a parking spot and sat there, and I cried and cried. Ten years for this. Ten years for nothing. Ten years down the drain. I didn't know what to do. About ten minutes later, I finally stopped crying. I wiped my eyes and said, 'I know what I have to do. It's the only way out, the only solution.'" Josh paused. His crying turn into loud sobs and tears were falling from his eyes. Everyone there was wide-eyed with expectancy.

"I got the picture out and I smiled. Then I said, 'Hello Aunt Sue, Uncle John, Jared and Jason. I'm sorry, but I have to tell you this is the last time I'll be talking to you. I will miss our nightly talks. I love you guys so much but I can't take this anymore. I tried, oh god, how I tried for ten years. I'm so sorry, but I know the only way out of this misery is to end it all. I can't go on living this life anymore. I want you to know that I love all of you so very much. So goodbye Aunt Sue, goodbye Uncle John, goodbye Jared, goodbye Jason. I love you.'"

Josh was sobbing loudly and heavily as he spoke those words. Aunt Sue, Jared and Jason were also audibly crying. Uncle John and the two lawyers had tears streaming from their eyes. Between sobs, Josh said, "I'm so sorry," pause, more sobs, ". . . . I . . . I feel . . . so . . . ashamed." Pause. Sobs.

"Aunt Sue . . . Uncle John . . . Jared . . . Jason," pause, sobs. ". . . I . . . I . . . was going to . . . kill myself."

It took nearly a minute for Josh's sobs to cease. He was then breathing heavily. Aunt Sue said, "It's all right, Josh. You're here now, you're safe and you have a family now and a home. You don't have to worry about anything anymore. Josh, do you want to stop?"

"No, Aunt Sue. I'll be all right. I want to finish." Josh then told everyone about going to a hotel to think about everything, going to the cafe, ordering soup while staring at the picture, how rude he was to the guy who asked if he could help, the unexpected hamburger and about finding the guy to apologize, then reading the memoir and telling the guy some of his problems.

Josh said, "Aunt Sue, Uncle John, Jared, Jason, this guy Mark turned out to be my Clarence, like in the movie, 'It's a Wonderful Life'. He became my guardian angel. He saved my life! He did so much for me. He paid for my rooms and paid to get my car fixed and that cost almost $1,500. With the dinners," Josh told them about the duck, escargot, crème broulee, raw oysters, octopus and the stuffed lobster tails, "and water and jets ski rentals, he had to have spent over $3,000. When I got to Key West, I had $211. Now I have $1,011. When I left, he insisted on giving me $800. I love him so much."

Jared spoke up, "Wow, I'd like to meet this guy."

"Yeah, me too," cried out Jason.

It was Uncle John's turn, "So would I. Perhaps we can ask him to come here to visit."

Josh said, "I asked him that, and he said he would come."

Aunt Sue asked, "Josh, is there anything else you would like to tell us?"

"Well, there is one more thing. I won't be eighteen until next month so I don't know if I have to wait. I want to get emancipated from my parents. And if possible, I want to change my name. I don't want anything to remind me of them. I don't want to think about them anymore, and I don't want to talk about them anymore. If possible, I'd like to do this right away."

John looked at William Stafford and said, "Bill?"

"Based on what I heard, this is definitely possible. We could file a petition for emancipation and for a name change. How long it would take depends on whether the parents file an objection or not."

Josh said, "Yeah, they'd probably do that just for spite."

Aunt Sue asked, "Josh, what do you want to change your name to?"

"Well, I was thinking, but if think it's a bad idea, just tell me. I'd like to use your name . . . Brennan."

Aunt Sue almost shrieked, "That is a great idea. It would make us so happy. What about your first name?"

"Well, they gave it to me, so I'd changed that too."

Uncle John spoke out, "Josh, it's not just a coincidence that the names of the males in this family start with the letter J. Your parents did not give you the name. When you were born, we asked your mother what she was going to name you. She said she didn't care and told us to pick a name, so your Aunt Sue and I named you. Don't ask why she didn't want to name you."

"You did? I never knew that. Gee, in that case I want to keep it. And you don't have to tell me why. I already know. They told me often enough they wished I was never born."

Jason then shouted out, "WAIT, WAIT. You're going too fast for me. What's emancipated mean?"

Bill Stafford replied, "That means Josh's parents would have no rights as parents, so they, in effect, would not legally be his parents anymore."

Jared looked at Jason and Jason looked at Jared who nodded his head to the right meaning he wanted to talk to Jason alone.

Jared stood, "Jason and I have to talk. We'll be right back."

Jason added, "And don't say anything until we get back. We don't want to miss anything."

Bill Stafford said, "Yes sir."

In another room, Jared said to Jason, "Are you thinking what I'm thinking?"

Jason happily said, "Yeah, adoption." To which both boys shouted out in delight.

When they returned, each person stared at the boys with puzzled looks. Uncle John said, "That certainly was a short and happy conference. Are you going to clue us in?"

Jared responded while looking at Bill Stafford, "If Josh gets emancipated, I guess that means he doesn't have parents anymore."

Bill nodded in agreement. Jared said, "Well, we don't think it's right. Go ahead Jason, tell them."

Looking at his mom and dad, Jason said, "Yeah, it's not fair that Josh won't have parents. So mom and dad, we want you to adopt Josh. That way he *will* have parents."

Jared added, "And we'll have a big brother instead of only a cousin."

Aunt Sue excitedly said, "What a great idea! We would love that."

Uncle John said, "Jared, Jason, you two are something special."

All eyes turned to Josh who had a shocked look on his face. Aunt Sue said, "Josh honey, would you like us to adopt you?"

Josh looked at his aunt, his uncle and then his two cousins. He blurted out, "I can't let you do that."

A chorus of '*whats*' and '*why nots*' was heard, to which Josh, with new tears in his eyes, said, "You don't even know me. Suppose you don't like me?"

Aunt Sue replied, "Josh, we know we love you. We always thought of you as our third son and now we want to make it legal."

Jason said, "Please say yes, Josh."

Jared added, "We both want you to be our brother. Please?"

More tears from Josh, "If you really want me to, I'd be the happiest person on earth."

He stood up, went to his would-be brothers and in a low voice said, "Group hug."

As the three boys hugged each other, Josh said, "I love you guys. Thank you." Josh then went to his aunt and uncle, hugged them and told them the same thing.

Uncle John looked at his lawyer, "Well, Bill, what do you think?"

Bill Stafford replied, "Emancipation, name change, adoption. We really have our work cut out for us." He said this looking at Daniel Conway.

"We'll get on this right away. We may have enough to have the court put this on a fast track. I have a few ideas on how to make this happen. Since Josh is still a minor, I have to cover all bases so I will have to contact the Child Protective Service. But don't worry, Josh, this is a mere formality. You're not going anywhere."

Bill continued, "There is one more thing. These matters will be decided in a court of law by a judge and we're going to need the support of the CPS. It would give us a stronger case if we can submit this tape to the judge and the CPS Social Worker. Both would be bound by confidentiality, the same as your lawyers are. So what I am going to ask you, Josh, would you give us permission to submit this tape to the judge and the CPS Social Worker? No one else would ever see it."

"Mr. Stafford, I trust you. I don't care who sees the tape. You can show to anyone you want. So yes, you have my permission."

Mr. Stafford thanked Josh.

Aunt Sue asked, "Josh, honey, do you think you need to talk to a professional about all this?"

"No, Aunt Sue. I have Mark to talk to and no one can be better than him. Besides, I have all of you and that's all I need. I'll be fine."

After Bill asked Josh several questions, including information about his parents, where they lived and their daily habits, he stood and said, "We have what we need. I'll be in touch, John." He then went to Josh and said, "You are a remarkable young man, and I feel privileged to be able to represent you."

Josh thanked him and gave him hug and then went to Daniel and thanked and hugged him.

As they were leaving, Bill turned to his associate, "Daniel—"

But Daniel interrupted and said, "I know, what time tomorrow?"

Bill said, "We have a lot to do. How about 9:00 a.m.?"

"Fine, and I'll call Sandra to see if she can make it. We'll need her." Bill said, "I'll say we do. We have to file petitions for emancipation, a name change and the big one, adoption. She is a great paralegal. On Monday, I'll call the CPS. And Daniel, when all this is over you can count on a bonus because of this case. And tell Sandra she also will be up for a bonus."

"Wow, thank you, Bill."

After the two lawyers left, the Brennans and Josh took a break. The boys had sodas and Sue and John had coffee. Uncle John told Josh that he was going to put Josh's cell phone on the family plan. He also said that he and Aunt Sue thought it was a good idea for Josh to see the family doctor for a physical, and then their dentist. Josh agreed to that. Aunt Sue asked, "Josh, how do you feel now that you told us about the past?"

"You know, Mark was right. I feel like a great big weight was taken off my shoulders. I really think that my past is something I will never think about again. I really feel great, mentally and emotionally."

Jared spoke up, "Mom, I think the first thing Josh needs to do is go out and buy some clothes. He doesn't have much."

Josh said, "Yeah, you're right about that. Is there a Walmart around?"

Both Jared and Jason shouted, "WALMART? NO WAY."

Josh asked, "Target?"

"No WAY."

"Where then?"

Jared replied, "Navy or A&F or places like that. Josh, do you want to go now? Mom, dad, Jason and I can go with him."

Josh looked at his aunt and uncle. Aunt Sue said, "That's a wonderful idea. You have plenty of time. Dinner will about six thirty or so."

Jason said, "Come on, Josh. Let's go."

Uncle John held up a hand and said, "Whoa, Whoa. Josh can't drive his car until we get it registered on Monday and get him insured."

Jared said, "Oh . . . sorry. I forgot."

Uncle John said, "No problem. I'll take you guys and when you get done, call and I'll pick you up. And Josh, I want you to use my credit card and there's no limit to what you can spend."

"Thank you, Uncle John, but if you don't mind I rather pay myself. After all, I do have over $1,000. I'd feel better about it. And then I can tell Mark what he bought me. He'll be so happy."

Uncle John agreed.

At the mall, the boys were done shopping, and it being summer, there were great sale prices. They purchased slacks, shirts, shorts and footwear, all casual, plus smaller purchases like toiletries, underwear and other things Josh would need.

Jared said, "I guess we can call dad now."

Josh said, "Not yet Jared. I only spent about $500. Now I want to buy you guys something."

"No way." Jared said.

Josh was adamant and said, "Yes, way. We are not leaving until I get you something. Now what do you guys want?"

Jared, sensing that Josh's buying them something would make him happy, said, "Okay, Josh, how about a video game?"

Josh said, "Fine, one for each of you." They went to the video store and Jason got so excited when he found a new game that he didn't have. Jared also got into the excitement. Josh had a big smile on his face as he watched them . . . and this did not go unnoticed by the two boys.

Josh then said, "Now I have to buy something for Aunt Sue and Uncle John. I was thinking of a bouquet of flowers for Aunt Sue. What do you think?"

Jared said, "She loves flowers. She's going to love you even more than she does now, if that's possible."

Josh said, "What can I get for Uncle John?"

Jason jumped in, "He loves some types of fancy gourmet sweets. Come on, the store's right over there."

When they got home, Josh was carrying the huge bouquet of flowers and a big box of gourmet sweets.

The boys were carrying the bags containing Josh's clothes. Aunt Sue screamed when Josh handed her the flowers, "These are so beautiful. I've never seen such beautiful flowers. But it's so big. Josh, you shouldn't be spending money on us." With tears in her eyes, she hugged Josh.

When Josh gave Uncle John his sweets, Uncle John's eyes bulged. With box in hand he hugged Josh, lifted him up and swung him around in a circle. "I know I should say you shouldn't have, but I'm glad you did. Thank you, son." When John heard the word "son" there were tears in his eyes.

Jared and Jason showed their parents the video games Josh bought for them and then began to empty the bags to show their parents what Josh bought. Josh was getting a kick at their excitement. Jason said, "And we picked out everything."

Jared added, "Yeah, Josh's fashion sense leaves a lot to be desired."

Everyone laughed.

Then Jared pulled out another bag and said, "This item is the most important one." He opened the bag and pulled a rather skimpy pair of Speedos.

Jason said, "Nice."

Aunt Sue and Uncle John laughed.

Josh, with a shocked look at what Jared was holding, said, "You don't expect me to wear that do you?"

Jared said, "We sure do."

Jason added, "This is so cool Josh."

"No way will I wear that. I'd be so embarrassed."

Jared said, "We both have a pair, so you won't be alone."

Uncle John piped in, "Josh, you're fighting a losing battle. I'm afraid you are now a member of Jason's and Jared's Speedo club."

Jason still very excited said, "And when you call Mark, don't forget to tell him about your Speedos."

Aunt Sue said, "All right, boys, break this up. Go up and put Josh's clothes away. Dinner will be in about a half hour. And don't forget to wash up."

The dinner consisted of Caesar's salad, leg of lamb, broccoli *au gratin*, and garlic and sour cream mashed potatoes. With practically each bite, Josh would say how delicious everything was. It was obvious to everyone around the table that Josh loved it.

During the dinner conversation, Aunt Sue said, "Josh, tomorrow we planned to have a barbecue party."

"Barbecue? I've never been to a barbecue before."

"You will love it. We all thought it would be a good idea to have you meet some people. So we've invited some of our close friends."

Jason excitedly jumped in, "And Jared and I invited some of our friends too. We'll have a great time."

"I don't know, Aunt Sue. I've never been with a group of people. I won't know how to act."

Uncle John said, "Just be yourself kiddo. They are all very nice people. They won't expect you to make a speech or perform." He chuckled.

Jared said, "Don't worry. We'll have fun swimming, playing volleyball and maybe video games. You will like our friends. They're all crazy, just like Jason."

"Hey, watch it bro."

"Okay. I'll try not to embarrass you."

"That, kiddo, is something you could never do."

After dinner when the table was cleared, Aunt Sue returned from the kitchen with a chocolate layer cake, and on top in white icing were the words, "Welcome Home Josh." Yup, there were tears in Josh's eyes. On the cake were five candles around the perimeter and one in the center, each with a small paper attached parallel to the cake.

Jason was so excited, he said, "Josh, read what's on the papers. Start here." Josh read them. The first candle read "Mom," the second, "Dad," then "Jared," then "Jason" and the fifth candle read "Josh." The center candle read "Our Family." Josh started to quietly cry.

"This is one of the most wonderful things I've ever seen. It means so much to me. Thank you so much. I love you all."

After the boys played a few video games, they decided to call it a night even though it was only ten fifteen. As Josh lay on his bed, he heard a knock on his door.

"Come in."

Jared and Jason walked in wearing only their shorts. Jared said, "Josh, we know you had a rough day, but we're so happy you're here. We were wondering . . . uh . . . uh . . . would it be okay if the three of us cuddled for a while?"

Jason added, "Please, just for a little while."

Josh smiled at the boys and said, "I would really like that."

At around 11:00 p.m., Aunt Sue walked upstairs to go to bed and noticed that both Jared's and Jason's bedroom doors were open. She looked in and neither boy was there. Puzzled, she looked at Josh's bedroom and saw the door was ajar. She peeked in, backed up, went to her room and said, "John, get your camera out, quickly."

Sue and John went to Josh's room and they saw the three boys fast asleep cuddled together with Josh in the center. John snapped a few pictures and they left.

The next morning, Josh walked into the kitchen where both Aunt Sue and Uncle John were.

Aunt Sue said, "Good morning Josh. Did you sleep well?" Josh told her it was the best night sleep he ever had. Jason and Jared came in. After a breakfast of waffles and sausage, Uncle John, with a smile on his face, put a framed picture on the table. All three boys looked at it and all three boys blushed.

Aunt Sue said, "You looked so cute we couldn't resist taking a picture."

Jason said, "You're not mad?"

His mom replied, "Mad? Of course not. I think it was a wonderful idea to cuddle like that."

Uncle John said, "I agree with your mom. I have a suspicion that Josh needed that. Josh, you look so at peace in this picture. I hope you don't mind the picture."

Josh said, "No sir, I don't mind and you're right, I did need that."

Uncle John said, "And boys, next time you want privacy in your bedroom, close your door." All three boys blushed again.

Aunt Sue said, "Boys, you have a couple of hours. I'll be busy this morning getting ready."

Josh said, "Aunt Sue, may I help you or Uncle John with whatever you're doing?"

"You don't have to do anything."

"But you don't understand. I want to help. I've never done anything like this before and I'd like to. I never had a mother or father to do anything with. And I'd like to learn even if I sit around and watch."

"In that case, both your Uncle John and I will put you to work. We'll try not to wear you out." She laughed.

Jason said, "Then I want to help too."

Jared said, "Yeah, so do I."

His dad said, "An all-time first . . . Jason and Jared volunteering."

Both boys shouted, "Daaad, you know that's not true." Uncle John agreed and said he was only joking.

Josh was having a ball helping Aunt Sue in the kitchen, peeling potatoes, chopping vegetables, making salads, washing pots and pans. Jared and Jason were loving it as well. The three boys went outside to help Uncle John. It was then that Josh looked up and saw the banner, the same one as yesterday, but this time it was hanging on the rear of the house. He stared at it for a few seconds and then went to work setting up tables and chairs, then getting the barbecue grill ready. For the first time in his life, he felt useful, and for the first time, he was working alongside his family. He was so happy.

The guests began arriving around 1:00 p.m., many coming with plates or platters of food. Jared's and Jason's friends came shortly after one o'clock, four of Jared's friends and three of Jason's. Josh was introduced to the friends and they were all happy to meet him. Those nine boys then got into a huddle which Josh thought was really neat. The huddle broke up and they shouted, "Let's get him!" They all charged at Josh, lifted him up and threw him into the pool. Each of the boys followed and jumped in. All ten boys began the usual young boys' horsing around stuff. One of Jason's friends jumped up in the water and ended up sitting on Josh's shoulders. He yelled out, "Chicken fight!" Soon there were five teams of chicken fighters going at it. This lasted about twenty minutes when exhaustion set in. Jared then declared, "Josh, you are now initiated." The rest all cheered.

When all the guests arrived, there must have been fourteen excluding Jared's and Jason's friends. Aunt Sue walked with Josh, introducing them. They were all very friendly and they wished him luck and happiness in his new home. Josh wasn't as unconformable as he thought he would be. After they made their rounds, Jason came running up and told Josh they were starting a volleyball game. Although Josh had never played before, he got the hang of it and had a lot of fun.

After the game, Josh went to get a soda and he saw Aunt Sue talking to a couple with their son who was sitting on his mom's lap. He heard the boy's mother say, "He's still very shy. We can't get him out of his shell. He's still afraid to play with children his age. Even our child psychologist isn't helping." Josh looked at the boy who looked to be four or five years old. He was leaning against his mom with his arm around her shoulder.

Josh walked over to them, knelt down by the boy and said, "Hi, my name is Josh. What's your name?"

The boy said nothing and hugged his mom tighter.

"Won't you tell me your name?" No response.

"I know your name, it's Tickle Me Elmo." Josh tickled the little boy who gave a giggle.

"No? Then it's Big Bird." Josh waved his arms in the air as if flying.

"Then it must be Mickey Mouse."

"Donald Duck?"

"I know what your name is. Your name is mommy."

Finally, the boy looked at Josh and said, "No, silly. This is my mommy."

"If your name is not mommy, what is it?"

"I'm Bobby."

"Hi, Bobby. Bobby, I have no one to play with. Will you play with me?" No response.

"Bobby, if you don't play with me, I'm going to cry." Josh put on his saddest face.

"Don't cry," the boy pleaded.

"I know, we can play horsey."

"Horsey? What's that?"

"Stand up and I'll show you."

The boy stood and Josh turned him around so that he was facing away from him. "Now, spread your legs like this. Are you ready?" Bobby said he was. Josh lifted him up in one quick swoosh and Bobby was sitting on Josh's shoulders. Josh said, "Now I'm the horsey and you're the cowboy." Josh glanced at Bobby's parents who both were looking with an amazed look on their faces.

"To ride the horsey you have to say 'Giddyap.'"

Bobby said, "Giddyap."

"Louder, you have to shout so your horsey can hear you."

Bobby shouted, "GIDDYAP." With that command, Josh began trotting around the yard slowly and with a hop to his step. As they passed his mom and dad, Bobby yelled, "Look mommy, I'm riding the horsey."

After a few laps, Josh told Bobby that to stop the horsey he had to yell, "Whoa, horsey."

Bobby said, "Whoa, horsey."

"Louder, the horsey can't hear you."

"WHOA, HORSEY," and Josh stopped.

They walked to Bobby's mom and dad both of whom had tears in their eyes.

"Mommy, daddy, did you see me ride the horsey? It was so much fun." They both hugged their son.

Bobby's dad turned to Aunt Sue who was watching the whole thing and said, "You never told us that Josh can work miracles."

Josh whispered in Bobby's mom's ear, "Can I take him in the pool?"

"Absolutely, if you can get him in it. I doubt you could. For some reason, he's afraid of pools."

So Josh said, "Bobby, do want to go in the pool with me?"

"No, I'm scared."

"But I'll hold you tight, and then you can splash me and dunk my head in the water. Come on, it'll be fun."

He took Bobby's hand and when they got to the pool, he lifted the boy up and carried him into the pool. In the pool, he turned Bobby in circles, lifted him up and down, and Bobby kept laughing and screaming in delight. By this time, everyone was standing by the pool watching.

Jared, Jason and their friends swam up to where Josh and Bobby were playing and Jason said, "Hey, we want to play too." For the next fifteen or twenty minutes, all the boys were playing with Bobby.

When the play ended, Josh said to Bobby, "Do what I'm doing." Josh's arms were moving in swim stroke fashion. Bobby started.

Josh said, "Slower, like this. Good, now stretch your arms. Good, just a little faster. Perfect."

Josh then laid Bobby on his stomach and put his hands on Bobby's stomach and said, "Keep moving your arms."

Josh walked as Bobby kept stroking. After a minute or so, Josh took one hand away and raised it in the air while still walking.

Bobby said, "This is fun."

After another minute or so, Josh very slowly lowered the hand that was on Bobby's stomach and much to his own amazement, Bobby was actually swimming on his own. Suddenly, Josh took that hand out of the water and raised it in the air so everyone could see

Bobby swimming. When Josh saw that Bobby was tiring, he grabbed a hold of him and lifted Bobby to his chest. The crowd watching started to clap and cheer.

"Look Bobby, everybody is cheering for you."

Josh carried Bobby back to his parents. "Mommy, Daddy, did you see me swim?"

"Yes, dear, you were wonderful. Come, let's get you dried off and then we'll have something to eat."

Bobby's dad said to Josh, "Thank you Josh. You just did what no one was able to do for our boy. We've never seen him have so much fun. I wish I can repay you somehow."

Josh replied, "No, playing with Bobby was enough. I have to tell you, Bobby probably helped me more than I helped him. I guess you know what I mean."

"I think I do. I hope we'll see you again and if there anything we can do for you, let us know."

As the barbecue was winding down, Josh noticed that Bobby's parents were getting ready to leave. So he went to them. He heard Bobby say, "I don't want to go. I want to stay with Josh."

Josh said, "Bobby, I have to go too. I'll tell you what. I'll come to your house soon and we'll play again. Okay?"

"Promise?"

"I promise." Josh told Bobby's parents that he'd call when he could make it.

The boys insisted that the two parents go inside and relax and that they would clean up. They were done at about nine thirty. The boys were so tired, they had a light snack and went straight to bed.

That same day, Sunday, William Stafford, Daniel Conway and Sandra met at 9:00 a.m. in the law office.

He explained how they were going to proceed and what needed to be done. Daniel would start on the petitions while Sandra would research previously adjudicated cases that could possibly be a precedent. "The first thing I have to do is make a phone call. A colleague of mine has his law practice in the same town where Josh's parents live and I want to see how well connected he is . . . with the police.

When I'm through, I'll work with Daniel on the petitions. Daniel, why don't you start with the emancipation petition, but before you do, make four copies of the tape. Sandra, if you need help researching adjudicated cases give a shout. We need to get this done today."

During breakfast on Monday morning, Josh said, "Aunt Sue, Uncle John, I'd like to talk to you about college. If possible, I would like to go if I can get accepted and if I can afford it. Mark said there must be a community college someplace around here."

Uncle John said, "I glad you brought this up. Your Aunt Sue and I briefly discussed it and we were going to ask you to consider it. Guess we don't have to do that now. Yes, there is a two-year community college not far from here, Browning County College. It is a great way to get started and it would be an easy adjustment for you to make. But let's get one thing straight right now. Regardless how the court cases come out, you are now one of the family. We consider you to be our son and we intend to treat you the same way we treat Jared and Jason. When, not if, but when you go to college, you are not paying, we are. Just like we will be paying Jared's and Jason's college. And that's final."

"Gee, I don't know what to say. Thank you, Uncle John. Aunt Sue, do you think I can get accepted? My grades weren't all that hot."

"I *know* it won't be a problem. Josh, I'm a teacher and I know many students who went to Browning with less than average grades. I'll make an appointment for you to meet with a counselor at the school. And I'll go with you so we can see what we need to do. I am absolute thrilled that you will be going to college."

"Thanks, Aunt Sue. There are two more things. Would it be okay if I looked for a job? I don't want to spend every day doing nothing. And what chores can I do around the house. I want to feel that I am contributing."

Uncle John said, "Oh, don't worry about chores. You will get plenty of them. Just ask the boys. And as far as getting a job, by all means do that. You know what they say . . . work is good for body and soul. At least I think somebody said that. Oops, I'm running late. Have to get to work. See you later."

On Monday, Daniel and Sandra arrived at the office at 8:00 a.m. where they found Bill on the phone. When he was done, he said, "Step one of the plan is done. We will have a police escort to Josh's parents' house. One of the policemen that my colleague knows well is coming. His name is Doug and he will follow us there. We'll leave here at about nine thirty to meet up with him. Now I am waiting for a call from Jennifer Marlowe of the CPS. I met her once and I remembered being impressed with her."

Sandra said, "While we're waiting, I have a couple things I want to check out."

Daniel said, "Same here."

The phone rang at eight forty. "Hello, Jennifer."

"I can't believe I'm talking to the most esteemed lawyer in the state, maybe the country."

"Thanks, Jennifer. Listen, I'm pressed for time and I need your help." Bill gave a condensed version of Josh's life, about his parental abuse and his struggle for survival. He then told her about the emancipation, the name change and the adoption plans. "He's seventeen and will be eighteen in about a month, but there is an urgency to this matter. I want to cover all the bases before I file the petitions and that's why I called you. I have a video tape of Josh telling his story and I'd like you to watch it. He did give me permission to share it with you. It's about thirty minutes long and it will explain everything."

"Yes, I can do that."

"But, Jennifer, I would like to file the petition tomorrow morning. So if you can finish up on your end today, I'll be able to file. Jennifer, once you see this video, I know you will see the urgency and you will want to get this done quickly as much as I do. One caveat however. When you watch the tape, make sure you have a box of tissues handy."

"That bad, huh?"

"Oh yeah. I assume you'll want to meet with Josh and his aunt and uncle, so maybe we can arrange it for this afternoon. That is, if you have the time."

"I'll make the time. How soon can you get the tape to me?"

"I'll send it by messenger service. You will get it within the hour, and Jennifer, no one else, okay?"

"Gotcha."

"I should be done with what I have do before noon so I'll call you later. And thank you, Jennifer."

When he got off the phone, Daniel and Sandra were waiting for him. "Okay, time to leave."

Daniel said, "Let's do it."

Bill, Daniel, and Sandra slowly pulled up to the parents' house with Doug in his patrol car right behind them. After Daniel parked, he, Bill and Sandra walked to the door. Bill knocked, waited a few seconds and knocked harder. As he was ready to knock again, the door opened and a woman whom Bill assumed was Josh's mother said, "Yeah? What do you want?"

Bill introduced himself, then Daniel and Sandra. He asked if Josh was her son and she nodded.

"We are representing your son, Josh, and we would like to speak to you and your husband."

A male voice yelled out, "Who's at the door?" Bill knew this was the father.

"Some lawyers wants to talk to us about Josh."

The father came to the door, "We don't want to talk to you or anybody about that no good brat."

"Listen, Mr. and Mrs. Armstrong, we can do this the easy way by talking now or I can cause you major problems. And believe me, I will and you will not like it one bit."

"All right, all right, come in but make it fast."

Once inside, Bill said, "I am representing Josh. But let me make this clear. He does not know we are here. I'll get straight to the point. There are two things I want from you and when I get both, you will never see us or hear from us again."

"Whaddya want from me. I can't give you anything."

"We know a lot about Josh and how he lived when he was with you. We also know that you neglected your parental responsibility—"

"Wait, wait, hold on here."

"No, you wait. Let me finish. I think you are going to agree with me and like what I have to say."

"Okay, okay, let's get this over with. Whaddya want from us?"

"As I said, two things. First, I want you both to sign this statement in which you relinquish or give up all your parental rights and claims. The result of signing this would mean, in effect, that legally you will no longer be Josh's parents."

"I know who put you up to this . . . Sue. She's a b—h."

"Who is Sue?"

"You don't know her?"

"How am I supposed to know her?"

"I guess you don't. What's the second thing?"

"We know what Josh's life was like for the past nine years or so. We know that you neglected and ignored him and didn't even provide him with food or clothing. He lived in misery during this time but managed to survive totally on his own." The father started to say something, but Bill stopped him.

"We think Josh's years of torment are worth something, and that he should be compensated because of this. You had never contributed to his past well-being but now we expect you to contribute to his future well-being."

"What the hell are you talking about?"

"Compensation. We think a fair amount is $2,000 for each year of suffering. That's $18,000, but since I'm such a nice guy, I'll make it $15,000 that we expect you to give us for Josh's future. After that, we'll be out of your life forever."

"You're out of your mind. I don't have $15,000 and even if I did, I wouldn't give you a penny. Now get out of my house."

"Listen very carefully, you sorry piece of trash. I'm sure you know how police have their informants to get information. Lawyers have their informants as well. I know what you have hidden in your bedroom closet, the stacks of money and the stacks of drugs. I also know about how much money you have hidden."

The father said, "What? What did that lying little brat tell you?"

Bill responded, "When I spoke to Josh, his exact words to me were, 'I don't want to think about them and I don't want to talk about them'."

"If it wasn't the brat, then who . . . "

Bill interrupted, "I am not going to tell you who my informant is, but still being a nice guy, I'll just say be careful who you're selling that stuff to."

"You no good son of a b—h. You expect me to give you everything. What do I get?"

"Your freedom." Bill paused to let this sink in. "Take a look out your window. If I open the door and wave to the police officer, he will come in, search your house, find your drugs and bring you both to jail."

"You need a search warrant for that."

"Oh, come on now, do you really think I would come unprepared?"

For the first time, Josh's mother spoke, "Victor, give him what he wants. I'm not going to jail."

"How do I know you won't come back for more?"

"First, you have my word. But more logically, if I wanted more I would have asked right now. I know you have at least three or four times the amount we're asking. You wouldn't even miss it."

"And the police?"

"I won't say a word to him about this. So far he doesn't know about the drugs but unless you agree, he will know."

"Mary, go get the money."

When she returned she gave the stack to Bill who then handed it to Daniel and Sandra and he nodded. They went to a table and counted. They returned and nodded.

Bill then got out the parental release statement and explained, "Sandra is a notary public so this statement will be a legal document. I need two witnesses. Daniel is one and I have to call the officer in to be the other. Don't worry, he will just sign and leave."

"Okay, let's get this over with."

They called Doug in. Bill had them sign five copies. The parents and witnesses signed and Sandra notarized each. No one said a word. When the group left, again not a word was spoken either by Bill or the parents.

Once outside, Daniel said, "Wow, you don't mess around do you? I think I learned more today than all my years in law school. I don't believe you pulled off that warrant bit."

Bill replied, "Hey, I never lied to the man."

Doug added, "I think I know what was going on in there. If I ever need a lawyer, I'm calling you." They all laughed and headed back home.

On the way back to the office Bill called Jennifer. It was now close to eleven fifteen, and he was hoping she viewed the tape.

"Hello, Jennifer. We're finished with what we had to do and we're on our way back to the office. How did you make out?"

"I watched the tape and let me tell you, this is the saddest story I've ever heard about. In the twelve years or so that I've been doing this, I've dealt with probably hundreds of youngsters, saw how they lived and how bad their lives were, but this is the saddest by far."

"I suppose you now know how badly I want to help the boy, and pronto. This cannot wait."

"I totally agree with you. So let's take the next step. I do need to meet with the boy and his entire family. How soon can we do that?"

"I'm sure I can get them all together this afternoon. Sue is a teacher so she's off for the summer. And John owns a successful investment firm, so since he's the boss he can do anything he wants. I'll ask Sue to call John and round up the boys. Is 3:00 p.m. good with you?"

"That would be perfect. I just have a few reports to do, but I'll have them done by then. And I can't wait to meet Josh."

"Great. I'll call Sue now and then I'll call you back to confirm."

On Monday morning, Aunt Sue and Josh went to the Motor Vehicle Center and registered his car. When they returned home, she called her insurance agent and put Josh's name on their family policy. She then received a call from Bill Stafford. "Hello Sue. This is Bill. The reason I am calling is that I spoke to the CPS Social Worker.

Her name is Jennifer Marlowe. She is a very nice person. She viewed the tape and wants to meet with you, John and Josh, and Jared and Jason as well."

Sue asked when and Bill replied, "She'd like to come today at about 3:00 p.m. Can you ask John to be there? And could you round up the boys?"

"John will be here and so will the boys. Is there anything we need to do?" After Bill told her no, they bid their farewells.

Sue immediately call John and told him about the 3:00 p.m. meeting and he said he would be there. He asked, "Are the boys around?"

"Yes, the Speedo group is at the pool."

"Really? Did they get Josh to wear one of those things?"

"I really don't know dear. I was doing some sewing in the den when I heard the thunder of footsteps racing down the stairs. Then Jason yelled, 'Mom, Speedo alert, no peeking'. Now you know we're not allowed to peek, but I must say I was tempted. Hopefully, they'll tell us if they convinced him."

"I would like to know myself. I hope they did. Someday I *am* going to peek and take a picture of the Speedo club." They both laughed and John said, "Honey, I have to run. I'll see you later."

When the boys came in with a towel around their waists, Sue had lunch prepared. Josh said, "Aunt Sue, I'd like to learn how to cook. I really enjoyed helping you yesterday. Could you teach me or I can just hang around and watch what you do?"

Aunt Sue replied, "Josh, that is an excellent idea. You can help me cook. That's the best way to learn. It will be a lot of fun."

Jared interjected, "Hey wait, if Josh is going to cook, I want to learn too."

Jason said, "Yeah, me too."

"Oh really? How come you never asked before?"

Jared laughingly replied, "Because Jason never thought of it."

Jason yelled out, "Me? Oh great, now it's my fault."

"That's enough boys. Just eat. Listen, Mr. Stafford is coming today at about 3:00 p.m. and he's bringing a social worker from the

CPS. She would like to talk to you Josh and I suppose she'll want to talk to the rest of us."

"Wow, that was fast. But I am a little worried about it."

"Josh, there is nothing to worry about. Mr. Stafford said the social worker is very nice. And don't forget, he said it was a mere formality."

"Yeah, I guess you're right."

"Of course I'm right. Now I want the three of you to give yourself enough time to take a shower. And I want you dressed and down here by two thirty in case they get here early. By the way Josh, did the boys convince you to wear the official Speedo club attire?" Josh's face turned beet red while Jared and Jason were moving their heads up and down, and Sue laughed.

John arrived home at about two thirty and the boys were already dressed and waiting. Bill Stafford and Daniel Conway arrived at about two forty-five. A couple minutes after three o'clock, the doorbell rang and John opened the door for Jennifer. In the living room, Bill introduced her to everyone. When she met Josh she said, "So you're Josh. I am very happy and honored to meet you. Please, give me a hug."

Jennifer then explained the procedures she was bound to follow since Josh was still a minor. She echoed what Bill had told the group by saying that in this case it was only a formality. She said she would be speaking to everyone individually. "First, I'd like to talk to Josh. Could you show me your room?" They went upstairs, and about thirty minutes later they returned . . . and Josh was smiling. She then spoke to Sue, John, Jared and Jason separately in the kitchen. Thirty minutes later, she said she had all the information she needed. Sue asked her if she would like to stay for dinner, but Jennifer, looking at Bill, declined saying she had to write a report.

Bill walked her to her car and asked her what she thought. Jennifer said she was so happy she was involved in this case and that she was going straight home to complete the report which would include her enthusiastic approval and recommendation supporting all petitions.

Bill asked, "Could I get the report early tomorrow morning? I'd like to file the petitions as early as possible."

"Bill, the courthouse opens at 8:00 a.m. I'd like to go with you. This is what I would suggest. We get there no later than seven fifty. We'll go to the office where you will file. I've been there many times and I know the person who will be receiving them. We're going to ask to speak to Judge Thomas Harding to request a speedy hearing."

"I've tried many cases before Judge Harding. He is very strict, but very fair. Good choice. Never met him personally."

"I have at several receptions and as strict as he is in the courtroom, he is as nice personally. I met his wife several times and she is priceless. I like them both. By the way, may I hold on to the tape in case I need it, although I don't think I will." Bill said yes and they agreed that Jennifer would arrive at his office with the report at 7:30 a.m.

Bill went back to the house and said there is one more matter that he had to take care of. With that, Daniel got up and handed Bill a large manila envelope. "Josh, we went to see your parents today and without going into details about how we got it, here it is. This is a signed and notarized statement that states both of your parents have given up all legal claims and rights as parents. This means, legally they are no longer your parents. This will certainly bolster our case."

"Wow. How did you do that?"

"Let's just say I gave them a really good reason."

Daniel jumped in, "Josh, you should have seen Bill in action. He was amazing. Your parents didn't stand a chance. I would characterize the good reason as a good threat."

"I guess I really don't want to know. By the way, you never told us how much all this is going to cost. I have money saved."

"Absolutely nothing. This is *pro bono*."

John objected, "That is not necessary Bill. We expect to and want to compensate you for all you're doing."

"WAIT," cried out Jason. "What's *pro bono*?"

"*Pro bono* is when a lawyer works on and/or tries a case, he or she does it at no charge to the client. All lawyers do it, and I have many times. So it's settled John." John nodded and said thank you.

Bill told them what he and Jennifer were going to be doing tomorrow morning. He then said, "One last thing for now." He handed another manila envelope to Josh and said, "This is yours."

Josh opened the envelope, his eyes bulged out and he cried out, "What is this for?"

"I convinced your parents that they should compensate you for the years of abuse and neglect and the misery they caused you."

"I can't take this. It's dirty money!"

"Josh, how do you know that? Did you ever see either of your parents actually selling drugs?"

"Well, no. But where else could it have come from?"

"I don't know that it's dirty money either. For all I know, it could have come from hoarding all the disability checks they received. Heaven knows they didn't use it to buy you food or anything. Josh, stop making assumptions. Just take the money for your future. You certainly deserve it and I would think you earned it."

Josh was struggling. He turned and looked pleadingly at Uncle John. Seeing that Josh needed help, John said, "Josh, Bill is right. You don't know where the money came from, and as Bill said, you really deserve it. I strongly urge you to accept the money."

Josh hesitantly asked Mr. Stafford, "How . . . how much . . . is . . ."

Bill right away said, "Fifteen thousand dollars."

"Wow!"

Jason jumped up, "JOSH, YOU'RE RICH!"

"I'd rather give it to you and Aunt Sue."

"No, Josh. That money is yours, for your future."

"Okay, Uncle John, if you think I should."

Bill said, "All settled."

After Bill left, Jared said, "Hey mom, when do we start cooking?"

His dad asked, "We?"

His mom replied, "I'll explain later." Sue then assigned each boy a task. They eagerly began while their mom (and aunt) explained whatever she was doing, step by step. The boys were loving it.

John said, "Now I've seen everything."

At dinner, the boys were ecstatic as they talked about what they helped prepare.

John said, "Josh, that's a great deal of money, and I have a suggestion as to what you should do with it."

Josh nodded.

"As you know, I am a Financial Investment Planner, and I spend every day investing other people's money in stocks, bonds, mutual funds and the like. All they do is sit back and watch their portfolio grow over time. Well, what do you think?"

"Wow. That would be great if you would do that."

"Great, next week I'll take you to my office and explain everything to you."

"*Ahem*," Jared loudly blurted out.

"Yes Jared, you can come too. And before I hear another 'ahem', you are can come too, Jason."

Jared said, "Well, you know how interested I am in what you do."

"I know, Jared."

On Tuesday morning, Jennifer arrived at Bill's office at exactly 7:30 a.m. She, Bill and Daniel discussed how they would proceed at the courthouse. They decided that Jennifer would take the lead with the clerk who would be accepting the petitions since she knew her. They were only hoping that they could get to talk to the judge. They gathered all the materials and left for the courthouse.

They arrived five minutes early and were happy to see the clerk at her desk. The three went to the desk and Bill introduce himself, Daniel and Jennifer. The clerk whose name was Emma said, "I know Jennifer well since she's been in this office often enough, and I do remember Mr. Conway who has been here several times filing petitions. And Mr. Stafford, it certainly is a pleasure meeting you. Your reputation precedes you."

"Thank you, Emma, and I am happy to meet you as well. These are the petitions we would like to file, three actually, all the same case."

Jennifer took over, "Emma, this is a case of a seventeen boy who survived ten years of hell. There's a great urgency to this case. What we need is to talk to Judge Harding for five minutes. We would like to get this on a fast track."

"If you mean now, I doubt he would see you. He does not like to be disturbed before he goes to court."

"Please, Emma, call him and tell him I said it's an absolute emergency."

"Very well, but I don't think he will like it."

Emma made the call and told the judge that Mr. Stafford, Mr. Conway and Ms. Marlowe were in the office filing petitions, and that they would like five minutes of his time.

"Yes, I know that, but my gut tells me I think you should make an exception. Ms. Marlowe said this case is an emergency." She hung up the phone and said, "He's not happy but he will see you now, and he emphatically said five minutes."

Jennifer thanked her profusely and said, "Emma, I owe you big time for this." Bill said the same words.

In the judge's chambers, Judge Harding greeted them and said, "Counselor, this better be good. Jennifer, what is this emergency?" Jennifer nodded to Bill indicating he should take over.

Bill thanked the judge for seeing them and said, "This is a case of a seventeen-year-old boy who endured physical and mental abuse from his parents for ten years. And during that time he had to fend for himself since his parents didn't even provide food for him. As a result, those years were about his trying to survive, not knowing each day if he would have food to eat."

"Daniel and I just met Josh on Saturday and we heard him describe his life. His story was so heart-wrenching that we both knew then and there that we had to help him." As Bill said this his eyes began to tear up.

"In the interest of time, I'll just tell what we are doing. We have filed three petitions, one for him to be emancipated from his parents, another for a name change and the third is a petition for adoption. His aunt and uncle very much want to adopt Josh who is currently living with them."

"To support these petitions, we have a notarized statement signed by both parents relinquishing their legal standing as parents. Since he is a minor, I asked Jennifer to go through the process and I have her report and recommendation." Bill handed both documents to the judge. He continued, "But the most important piece of evidence is this tape of Josh explaining how he survived."

"Your Honor, what we will be asking, or begging, is for you put this on a fast track. The reason is that although the boy seems fine physically, emotionally he is a wreck. I believe that he is teetering on the brink of being emotionally harmed unless this is resolved quickly. We are hoping that you will have the time to watch the tape, and if you do I am certain you will grant our request."

"And the second request is if you decide to adjudicate these petitions, that it be in camera since he is still a minor."

The judge finally spoke, "Counselor Stafford, you certainly came here with all barrels loaded. You've tried cases in my courtroom many times. I have always admired your work and how prepared you always are. You've only know the boy for three days so I sense that you and Mr. Conway crossed the proverbial line of never getting personally or emotionally involved with a client." Bill and Daniel both nodded their heads.

"Jennifer, you also have been in my courtroom many times. I've always thought you were deliberate in your cases, taking the time to ensure you are doing the right thing. So one of the reasons I agreed to meet with the three of you is because you said it was an emergency. And that piqued my interest. Would you like to contribute anything here?"

"Yes, Your Honor. I guess I crossed the proverbial line also. I crossed it when I watched the tape of Josh telling his story. Your Honor, I also am begging you to watch it. And if I may so bold as to suggest that you take it home and view it with your lovely wife. I've spoken to Sara several times and I know she will love watching the tape. It's only about thirty minutes long."

"How much of a fast track are you thinking of?"

Bill replied somewhat timidly, "Uh . . . this week, Your Honor."

"This week? I don't know if that is at all possible. My calendar is quite full this week. Let me give all this some thought and we'll be touch."

Jennifer said, "Oh, there's one more thing." Turning to Bill she said, "You'd better give the judge the caveat."

Bill laughed and said, "When you watch the tape, make sure you have a box of tissues handy."

They left the judge's chamber ten minutes later and Jennifer said, "Bill, you were magnificent in there. I think we've got him."

Daniel said, "I agree. You were so convincing. I am amazed at how much I am learning from you."

"I hope you two are right. But if weren't for you, Jennifer, I would not have gotten that opportunity. How would you like a job as a lawyer?"

Tuesday at the house the boys were free all day so Jared and Jason asked Josh if he wanted to do anything special. Josh preferred spending a couple hours at the pool and the Jacuzzi.

Jason yelled out, "YAY! Another Speedo party!"

Josh said, "Oh no, not again."

Jared added, "Come on, it wasn't too bad yesterday."

"I guess not."

Jared asked Josh if it was okay with him if they ask their friends over, and Josh thought it was a good idea. He was thinking the younger boys should have their friends over instead of only him. Besides, their friends were nice and a lot of fun.

Later in the day, Aunt Sue asked the boys if they would like to barbecue for their dinner. They all shouted, "YES!"

Josh asked, "Could we do the barbequing?"

"I'm sure that your Uncle John will show you how to barbecue. I was thinking we'll have spare ribs on the grill and maybe bratwurst. Those will be easy for you to barbecue."

The boys did most of the grilling with Uncle John guiding them every step of the way. They also grilled zucchini and a kettle of baked beans. Everyone, especially Josh, raved about how delicious every-thing was. Uncle John said, "You boys did a terrific job. We're so proud of you." The boys were beaming.

On Wednesday morning at the law office, things were very quiet. Bill was especially quiet and he kept looking at the phone say-ing to himself, *Come on phone, ring.*

At about 10:00 a.m. the phone did ring. He quickly picked up the receiver, "Good morning, this is Stafford Associates. How may I help you?" Bill listened and after about thirty seconds, he said thank you and put the receiver back on the phone. He sat there with a big smile on his face, then jumped up knocking his chair over and screamed, "YES!"

Daniel came rushing into his office with a concerned look. Before Daniel said anything, Bill said, "That was the Courthouse. Judge Harding will hear our petitions Friday at 3:00 p.m." The two men shook hands uttering phrases of elation.

On Wednesday morning at 9:00 a.m., Sue and Josh left to go to the community college. When they arrived, they were greeted by the counselor with whom Sue made the appointment. In her office, Josh and Sue gave the counselor some of his background and the name of the high school he attended. The counselor said there shouldn't be a problem registering Josh. She said she would contact his last school and get a copy of his transcripts. She gave Josh the application form, several pamphlets with information about the school and a booklet of course offerings along with each course description. She then gave them a tour around the campus. She said that she should be get-ting Josh's transcripts within a couple of days and when she received them, she would call to make another appointment for Josh to select his classes.

They arrived home at about ten thirty and shortly after they arrived, the phone rang. "Hello, Sue, this is Bill Stafford. Are you sit-ting or standing? Then sit down, I have something to tell you. Judge

Harding's office called and he will be hearing the petitions on Friday at 3:00 p.m."

Aunt Sue screamed, then said, "That is so wonderful. I am so happy. Do you think he'll grant the petitions?"

Bill replied, "No guarantees, but I think we have a good chance."

Hearing the scream, the three boys came running down the stairs, and Jared, seeing tears in his mom's eyes, worriedly asked, "Mom, Mom, what's the matter? What happened" Jason and Josh also looked worried.

Aunt Sue held her index finger up, then said into the phone, "No, I think you should call him in case he has any questions. Yes, thank you so much, Bill."

She turned to the boys and said, "That was Bill Stafford and he said that Judge Harding will hear the petitions on Friday at 3:00 p.m." Jared and Jason cheered at the good news but Josh just stood there in shock.

Jared said, "Whoa. That was fast. Mr. Stafford is amazing."

Josh nervously asked, "What do we do now?"

Aunt Sue said, "Nothing, just relax till Friday. But there is one thing we need to do. Josh, we need to go out and buy you a suit for court on Friday."

"A suit?"

"Yes, and boys, I want you to go upstairs and try on your suits. You haven't worn them in a long time and I want to see if they still fit. If not, we'll buy you new suits."

Jason moaned, "Aw, Mom, do we have to?"

"It's either that or you can wear your Speedos to court. Now git. We'll go right after you guys have lunch. As a matter of fact, we'll go to a restaurant for lunch and then we'll go shopping. I'll call your dad to see if he can join us."

John did join them and they discussed Friday. But John, sensing that Josh was worried and probably scared, quickly changed the subject. He mentioned an amusement park that was an approximate forty-minute drive and asked the boys if they would like to go sometime. Jared and Jason were overcome with excitement and kept talking about it. Josh was enjoying the boys' enthusiasm.

After lunch they got a nice suit for Josh. The suits the boys had still fit them so Aunt Sue bought them (and Josh) some casual clothes instead.

When they got home from shopping, Aunt Sue took the mail out of the mail box and saw a Post Office express envelope addressed to Josh. She called Josh and told him he had mail. She handed Josh the envelop and he noticed it was from Mark.

He hurriedly opened the envelop, looked at the contents and said in disbelief, "Oh my god, oh my god." He was staring at a bank check in the amount of $5,000 with a note attached that read, "Good luck, Josh. Love, Mark."

He showed the check to everyone, and Jason cried out, "JOSH, YOU'RE RICH AGAIN!" Everyone laughed at the resident clown as Josh reached for the phone to call Mark.

All day Thursday, Josh seemed relaxed but somewhat subdued. The boys tried to keep his mind off the court hearing and were successful for the most part. Aunt Sue deliberately planned a dinner that had a lot of prep time and she also planned on baking a cake from scratch. She thought that this would keep all three boys busy for a couple of hours. She gathered the boys together and told them her dinner plans. She told the boys that she wanted them to prepare everything while she watched and checked what they were doing. This worked out better than she planned because for the next two and a half hours, the three boys did the prep work and were having a blast.

After dinner, Josh became very quiet. He looked like he was in a trance. Noticing this, Uncle John said, "Josh, stop worrying. Tomorrow it will be all over with. Try to relax."

Josh said, "I will, Uncle John. I think I'll turn in early tonight. Good night." Both Aunt Sue and Uncle John said good night.

On Friday morning, Josh walked into the kitchen. Aunt Sue said, "Good morning Josh, were you able to sleep well?"

"Well . . . yeah . . . kinda . . . but I'm okay."

Jared then said, "Josh, we have all morning so how about playing some video games or pool or ping-pong. We haven't done that too much. It'll be fun."

"Thanks, Jared. You're really something, you know that? I know you're trying to get me to not think about this afternoon, and I love you for it. So the answer is yes."

After breakfast, the boys went to play video games and didn't return until about eleven thirty. Aunt Sue asked if they were ready for lunch, and Josh replied, "Aunt Sue, I don't think I can eat anything now. I'm kinda of nervous and scared. My stomach is in knots. I'd rather just hang around and rest until we have to leave." Aunt Sue gave him a hug.

At 2:00 p.m., everyone was dressed and ready to go. They wanted to be at the courthouse by two thirty.

Before they left, Uncle John got his camera out and said, "I want to take a couple of family pictures before we leave since our three boys are dressed up for a change. Everyone come over here."

Uncle John positioned everyone, set the camera on timer and took about five pictures.

When they arrived at the courthouse, Bill Stafford and Daniel Conway greeted them. Bill spent a few minutes briefing them on what he thinks will occur. They entered the courtroom at two forty-five and took their seats. Josh sat to Bill's right. To Josh's right were Aunt Sue, Uncle John, then Jennifer. Sitting to the left of Bill were Daniel, Jared and Jason.

There were only three other people in the courtroom, the bailiff, a stenographer and a lady sitting on the side. Bill did not know who she was. Jennifer came over and whispered in Bill's ear, "That is the judge's wife. There is only one reason she is here . . . the video. Great news for us." Bill simply nodded.

At exactly 3:00 p.m., the bailiff cried out, "In the matter of petitions filed on behalf of Joshua Armstrong, this court is now in session. Judge Thomas Harding presiding. All rise."

Judge Harding entered the courtroom, sat down and said, "Please be seated."

"The case before me, in camera, are petitions filed on behalf of seventeen-year-old Joshua Armstrong. Present in the courtroom are Joshua Armstrong, his attorneys, William Stafford and Daniel Conway, and his social worker from the Child Protective Service, Jennifer Marlowe. Also present are his aunt and uncle, Susan and John Brennan with whom Joshua is now residing, and their two sons, Jared and Jason Brennan."

"Before I begin, Mr. Stafford," Bill stood, "I know this case is being heard in camera but I hope you do not mind if I made one exception." The judge looked at his wife.

"No objection, Your Honor. In fact, we are happy she is here."

"Thank you, Counselor. I have read all your petitions and your support materials, and I must commend you for being so thorough."

"Thank you, Your Honor."

The judge continued, "Joshua Armstrong," Bill motioned for Josh to stand, "I will now ask you a few questions for the record. Is it your desire to be emancipated from your biological parents?"

"Yes, it is, Your Honor."

"Is it also your desire to legally change your surname from Armstrong to Brennan?"

"Yes, it is, Your Honor."

"Is it your desire to become the adopted son of Susan and John Brennan?"

"Yes, it is Your Honor, more than anything in the world."

"And finally, do you testify that you made these requests on your own and with no external pressure?"

"Yes, Your Honor."

"Please be seated." Josh and Bill sat.

"Ms. Jennifer Marlowe, please stand. For the record, please state your name and position." Jennifer responded. "Also for the record Ms. Marlowe, do you testify that the report and recommendations you filed in court are, in your professional opinion, both accurate and true?"

"Yes, Your Honor."

"Is it your professional opinion that these recommendations are the best recourse for these petitions?"

"Yes, Your Honor."

"Do you foresee any mental or emotional harm that could be suffered by Joshua?"

"No, Your Honor. On the contrary, the recommendations I offered would, in my opinion, be highly beneficial to his mental and emotional well-being."

"Thank you. You may be seated."

The judge continued, "I have before me the supporting materials presented by Counsel. I have read the report by Ms. Marlowe of the CPS and a notarized statement by Josh's parents relinquishing all legal claims of Joshua as their son. I also have a video tape of Joshua telling of his life for the past ten years, which I have viewed. By the way Counselor, thank you for your caveat. We both needed it." He looked to his wife, who smiled.

"Since Joshua's parents relinquished their rights as parents and because the CPS strongly supports the petitions before me, I see no reason why these petitions should not be granted."

With this announcement, neither Jared nor Jason could contain themselves. They jumped from their seats shouting, "ALL RIGHT!"

"WAY TO GO, JUDGE!"

"JUDGE, YOU'RE THE BEST!"

"THIS IS SO GREAT!"

The judge loudly rapped his gavel at the desk.

"Oops, sorry, Your Honor." Very embarrassed, they sat down with their heads hung low. They didn't notice the judge's grin and wink but Sue and John certainly did.

Looking at Jared and Jason, the judge said, "Would the two young and rather boisterous young men please rise." They stood.

"Please state your names." They both did, reluctantly.

"Gentlemen, this is a court of law where civility is maintained at all times. Those who know me know that I run a very disciplined courtroom. I do not tolerate such rambunctious behavior. When outbursts such as yours occur in my court, I always find the offenders in contempt and order them to spend a night in jail to calm down."

Jason, with a horrified look on his face, turned to his mom and dad, and in a trembling and high-pitched voice, he loudly cried out, "MOM, DAD . . . WE'RE GOING TO JAIL!"

His mom answered, "I know dear. We'll try to visit you."

Jason shouted, "TRY! WHAT DO YOU MEAN YOU'LL TRY!"

John got into the act, "That is, if we have the time."

Now Jared shouted out, "TIME! WHAT DO YOU MEAN IF YOU HAVE THE TIME!"

The grinning judge, enjoying the show, rapped his gavel again. The boys quickly turned to the judge who said, "Now, to the matter at hand, to wit, your sudden and very loud outburst. I have to admit that if I were in your shoes in anyone's courtroom, I would have reacted the same way, albeit not as exuberantly."

The judge then smiled, "I know that your reaction was rooted in your love of your soon-to-be brother."

Jason asked, "Does that mean we're not going to jail?"

The judge replied, "It does. Now if it's all right with you, may I continue and give my ruling?"

Jared said, "Sure, Judge, go right ahead."

Jason added, "Yeah, be our guest."

The judge smiled and said, "Why, thank you very much."

He asked Josh to rise. Josh and Mr. Stafford both stood. "The petition for emancipation is hereby granted. The petition for a name change is also granted. And finally, the petition for adoption is granted. This ruling will be sent to the appropriate government departments. You are now officially and legally the son of Susan and John Brennan, and your name is officially and legally Joshua Brennan."

Before the judge was able to continue, Jason shouted a loud "AHEM."

The judge, realizing why Jason did that, said, "Oh yes, you are also legally the brother of Jared and Jason Brennan." The smiling judge turned to Jared and Jason who gave the judge a thumbs up.

"Joshua, there is one nonbinding and optional condition to my ruling. It would please me very much if you would keep me informed as to how and what you are doing."

Josh replied, "I would like that very much, Your Honor. Thank you."

"Thank you, Joshua. The bailiff will give you my contact information when court is adjourned. But before I adjourn, I must say that I have never presided over a case that was so heart-wrenching, to borrow the term Mr. Stafford used when he told me about your case. It evolved into a heart-warming conclusion. I also never presided over a case that provided comedic relief," turning to Jared and Jason, "thanks to your rather enthusiastic brothers."

"Mr. and Mrs. Brennan, I must commend you for what have done for Joshua. I could almost feel the love that must abound in your family. And Mr. Stafford, Mr. Conway, Ms. Marlowe, I commend you also for taking such a personal interest in Joshua and for all that you did for him."

"Joshua, if at any time in the future I can be of assistance to you, please contact me. I feel very honored and privileged to have had the opportunity to preside over your case. You are a remarkable young man. Good luck, Joshua. Now give your parents and brothers a big hug. This court stands adjourned."

Josh turned to his parents, hugged them both and said, "Mom, Dad . . . my parents" as tears flowed from his eyes.

His mom also in tears said, "My son."

His equally teary-eyed dad said, "We love you, son."

Josh whimpered, "I am so happy."

Josh then turned to Jared and Jason who like everyone else had tears coming down from their eyes. He hugged them both and said, "Jared, Jason . . . my brothers." All three boys started crying.

Josh then said, "This is all your doing. You're the ones who thought of adoption. Thank you, bros. I love you so much."

Jared said, "We love you too, big bro."

Jason said excitedly, "Yeah, now I have two big bros."

Josh went to Mr. Stafford, Mr. Conway and Ms. Marlowe, thanked them and gave them hugs. Bill said, "You did it, big guy. Now you can think only about your future. If you ever need anything or just want to talk, let me know."

Daniel added, "Yes, Josh, please keep in touch with us." Jennifer echoed the same sentiments.

John approached them and said to Bill, Daniel and Jennifer, "How can we ever thank the three of you. Our thanks seem inadequate. Listen, we are going out to dinner to celebrate and we would like you to join us."

Josh added, "Yes, please come."

Bill responded, "Thanks, but no. Tonight is family night. You should spend your first night with family only. But how about if all of us go to dinner next week?"

Mrs. Harding then approached Josh. After introducing herself, she said, "Thank you for giving me the honor of viewing your tape. I was so touched that I had to come here today to meet you. I never come to court to watch any of Thomas's cases, but this time I felt compelled. I am hoping you will stay in contact with Thomas, and if you do, I would love to have you over for lunch or dinner some time."

"Mrs. Harding, I promise to keep in touch with Judge Harding, and I would very much like to see you again. Thank you."

On the way out, Jason suddenly stopped and shouted, "HEY, WAIT A MINUTE! WAIT A MINUTE! WAIT A COTTON-PICKIN' MINUTE!" Everyone stopped and looked at Jason.

"I just remembered. You guys said you'll try to visit us while we were in jail . . . on the chain gang . . . doing hard labor. What kind of parents are you?"

Jared jumped in, "Yeah, that's right. I can't believe our own parents would say that."

Their dad replied, "Relax boys. While your heads were hanging down almost to the floor trying to hide your embarrassment, the judge looked at us and smiled and winked. We knew he would be busting on you. We thought it was very funny."

Jason said, "Yeah, well . . ."

Jared said, "Well, it wasn't funny to us . . . but now that I think about it, it was kinda funny. I guess we'll keep you as parents."

But Jason was still sulking about it. Jared put his arm around Jason's shoulders, "Come on, little bro. So we were the butt of a joke, but you gotta admit it was funny that we both believed we were going to jail."

Jason thought a second, then said, "Yeah, you're right. It was funny. Okay, I'll let you guys stay our parents."

When the Brennan's returned from dinner, Josh said he had to call Mark to give him the good news.

When he was done with his call, Aunt Sue asked, "How do you feel? You must be tired after not sleeping much last night." Josh said he felt great. But his mom knew it was the adrenaline that was telling Josh he wasn't tired. When the adrenaline did wear off at about ten thirty, Josh suddenly felt exhausted. So he told everyone he was going to bed.

Josh left the door open while he put his clothes away. A couple of minutes later, Jared and Jason were at the door. Jared asked Josh if they could come in. The two boys sat on Josh's bed and Josh asked, "What's up bro's?"

Jason said, "Oh nothing."

Josh had a questioning look on his face and Jared said, "Come on, Jason. ask him."

"No, you ask."

"But it was your idea."

Josh had enough and said, "All right, guys, out with it."

Jared replied, "Well, you see, this is your first night here as our brother."

"Yeah?"

Jared continued, "So we were thinking . . . well . . . is it okay if . . . if we can . . . "

"All right, Jared, I got it. You guys want to cuddle." They both nodded. "But why all of a sudden are you afraid to ask?"

Jason said, "Well, we thought now that you have parents and that we're your brothers and that you'll have your own friends soon, you won't need us anymore."

Josh was shocked. "Oh my god, how can you ever think that? I love you guys and I always will. If it weren't for both of you, I wouldn't be here, much less have you as brothers. Even if I do have friends, you two will always be my best friends. I will always put you first, ahead of everyone."

Jason excitedly asked, "You mean that?"

"I mean it. Now, give me a hug. And I do want to cuddle, but under one condition."

"What's that?"

"That whenever you want to cuddle, just ask. I'll cuddle with you anytime, well, mostly every time."

"Thanks, Josh."

"Okay, now that we have that settled, go get ready. Oh, one more thing. I hope you will never be afraid of asking or telling me anything."

On Saturday morning Josh walked into the kitchen with a big smile on his face. He said, "Good morning, Mom. Good morning, Dad. Good morning, little bros, my two best-est friends. Ever since I woke up I couldn't wait to walk in here and say that to my new official and legal family."

The boys spent the morning doing chores around the house and in the yard. Josh enjoyed things like vacuuming, dusting, cleaning windows and especially working the yard. He was definitely feeling like he was contributing to his family.

After lunch which the boys prepared, Josh sat in a chair in the yard looking through the course descriptions from the community college. Jared and Jason were still in the house. At about 1:00 p.m. the doorbell rang and Jason went running to open the door. He knew it was his friend David and his older brother Scott. When Sue went to them, Jason introduced Scott to his mom who already knew David.

Scott said, "It's very nice meeting you Mrs. Brennan. I hope you don't mind my coming but David and Jason thought it would be a good idea if I met Josh since we're about the same age."

Aunt Sue smiled and said, "I think that's a wonderful idea. Scott, did the boys tell you anything about Josh?"

"Only that he's had a rough time before he moved here, nothing too specific."

"Just so you know, he may not want to talk about what he went through."

"I understand. Don't worry. It'll be okay. By the way, do you have anything special planned today? I'd like to ask Josh to come with me to meet some of my friends."

"No, nothing is planned, and I do hope you can convince him to go. He needs to be around people his own age. He is in the back yard reading. Just go through the french doors."

When Scott got to Josh he said, "Hey, how ya doing? My name is Scott." They bumped fists. "May I sit down?"

"Yeah, sure. I'm Josh."

"My brother is David, Jason's friend. He told me about you and how cool you are." Scott smiled like he was making a joke.

"David was here a couple times. Nice kid. But I don't know about the cool part."

"I came to welcome you to the neighborhood. What are you reading?"

"Just the course descriptions of the community college."

"You're going there? So am I. My first year."

"I'm hoping to go there."

"It would be cool if we had the same schedule. That way we can car pool. Take a look at my schedule." Scott took out his smart phone, pulled up his schedule and showed Josh.

"They're mostly required liberal arts courses, a couple of electives. Eighteen credits. I'll send you a copy on the computer." Josh gave Scott his email address.

Josh said, "I don't know too much about college or the courses. I'll be going next week to register and make out a schedule."

"Do you have any plans for the rest of the summer?"

"No, but Monday when I get back I'm going out to look for a job. I don't want to waste all this time doing nothing."

Scott stood up, pulled out his phone and said, "Be back in a minute. I gotta make a call." Scott walked about twenty paces, talked for about one minute and returned to Josh.

"Josh, you got a job."

"Huh? What do you mean?"

"You got a job with me. I work for a landscaper and we're swamped with work. I just talked to my boss and he asked how soon you can start. It's mostly mowing lawns, trimming bushes and branches, stuff like that, and he pays well. What do you say. Do you want the job?"

Josh excitedly and loudly said, "Yeah. Thank you Scott."

"No problem. My boss asked how old you were and I guessed seventeen. How old are you?"

"You were right, seventeen. I'll be eighteen next month."

"No kidding, me too. What date is your birthday?"

"August 22."

Scott jumped up and yelled, "No way, you gotta be kidding me!"

Hearing Scott yell, Jason, who was sitting with David across the yard, jumped up as if he were going to run to Josh's rescue. His mom saw Jason's reaction and said, "Jason, stay put."

Josh said, "No kidding. Why?"

"That's my birthday too. Wow, maybe we were destined to meet." He chuckled as he said that and Josh laughed as well.

Scott then asked, "How about your friends where you came from?"

"No friends. Never had a friend."

Scott said, "Josh, you have one now . . . me."

Sensing he made a mistake in bringing this up, Scott said, "Josh, I'm supposed to meet up with a couple of friends at the mall. How about coming with me. You'll like them. They're almost as nice as I am."

"Thanks, Scott, but I don't think so."

"Why not? You're not doing anything here. We'll have a lot of fun."

"Listen, Scott, I really appreciate your coming and being so nice and helpful and getting me a job, but I'm not too good around people."

"Josh, I'm really sorry. I didn't mean to . . . fine, if you won't go with me, then I don't go. I'll just hang around here with you."

Josh laughed and said, "In that case, I'll just go to my room and read."

"Fine, I'll just sit on the floor next to your door and wait."

"You're serious, aren't you?"

"Josh, listen to me for a minute. I don't know all that you went through. I just got bits and pieces of some of it. Correct me if I am wrong, but I'm kinda guessing that you went through hell. I heard it was about ten years. It seems to me that whatever it was, you were strong enough to overcome your problems, that you faced them with a steely determination. You probably got to a point where you feared nothing and no one. I'm guessing that you confronted the people who were responsible for your plight. You had to be strong, determined, unafraid and brave. But you won. And now you have a great family and the only thing you should be focused on is the future."

"Damn it, Josh. Sure, I came here feeling sorry for you. But after meeting you, there was no more pity. I liked you right away, and I just wanted to be your friend. I was on pins and needles trying to use the right words so I wouldn't upset you. You said you never had friends. Well, whether you want one or not, you have one now even if that friendship is not returned. What are you going to do? Shut out the world and the people in it. How long are you going to sit around feeling sorry for yourself?"

By this time, tears were falling from Josh's eyes. After a few seconds of silence, Scott said, "Josh, I'm really sorry. I was out of line for saying all those things."

Finally, Josh looked at Scott and said, "You are really something, you know that? You are absolutely right about everything you said. I am such a fool. I am the one who should be apologizing, not you."

"Does that mean you'll come with me to meet my friends?"

"Yes, but I'll have to check with Mom to see if she has any plans."

"No need, I already asked her . . . no plans."

"You are really something. Let's go."

When they walked inside, Jason asked where they were going. Scott said to the mall. When Jason asked if he and David could come, Josh turned to Scott indicating he should answer.

Scott said, "Not this time guys. Josh and I have some serious bonding to do."

Seeing their disappointed faces, Scott said, "Tell you what, next week we'll take you guys, okay?" Jason and David smiled happily and said that would be great.

When Josh's mom came into the room, Josh excitedly said, "Mom, guess what. Scott got me a job! It's a landscaping job and I'll be working with Scott."

Sue responded, "That is just wonderful. Thank you, Scott."

Josh said he had to go change clothes. After he left, Jason grabbed Scott by the hand and said, "Come on, we have to show you our game room."

When Scott and Josh found Scott's friends, he introduced them to each other. "Guys, this is Josh. He's new to the area. Josh, this is Eric and this is Brett."

They bumped fists and Scott asked, "Hey, where is Rob?"

"He went some place with his parents, I think to visit his grandparents."

Brett asked Josh, "So Josh, when did your family move here?"

Josh replied, "Well, I just arrived here last Saturday. I moved in with my aunt and uncle."

Eric said, "Huh? But what about your family? Where are they?"

Scott, knowing where this was headed interrupted, "Hey guys, let it go."

Eric said. "Let what go? I just asked where his family is."

Josh knew that Scott was trying to change the subject and was trying to protect him. He thought this wasn't fair to Scott. So he said, "Scott, it's okay."

Now Brett said, "What's okay? I don't get it. What are you guys talking about?"

Josh looked at Scott and said, "I know what you are doing. Thanks, but it's not necessary. I'll tell them."

"You don't have to do this."

"But I want to. I need to. It's not right or fair to all you guys if I don't."

Scott just nodded.

Josh gave them an abbreviated version of what his last six years were like, but did not leave out any of the sordid details that included his parents, being on his own, his struggles for survival, his thoughts of suicide and his guardian angel. He finished by telling them of the adoption.

As Josh was telling the boys about his life, there was only one person there without tears in his eyes . . . and that was Josh.

Josh then said, "So, guys . . . please . . . no pity, no sympathy. That's the last thing in the world I want or need because right now I am a very happy person."

Scott stood up and told Josh to stand. He gave Josh a hug and said, "This is not a hug of pity, it's one of my admiration and respect for you." Both Eric and Brett also gave Josh a hug.

Brett said to Josh, "Gee, you should write a book. You'd make a fortune."

Eric added, "Yeah, then we'll make it into a movie. I'll play Josh." Everyone laughed.

Scott then said, "All right, that's enough of this. What do you guys want to do?"

Eric said, "Let's leave it up to Josh since he's a new member of our group."

Josh said, "No, you guys decide. I've never done any social things."

Eric asked, "Hi-tech video games? Bowling? Movies?"

Josh shrugged, "Anything you want. I've never done any of those things. But I can try."

Scott said, "Since Josh is the new member of our very elite circle, it's our job to show him all the stuff he's missed. So how about we do all three of Eric's ideas. First, a few video games, then we'll bowl a couple of games, then we'll grab something to eat at the food court and then take in a movie."

Brett said, "Sounds like a plan. Let's go."

On the way to the video arcade, Scott said to Brett and Eric, "You guys should see the yard at Josh's house. It's unbelievable. They have a huge pool, a Jacuzzi, a net for volleyball and a half basketball court. And in their basement they have an amazing game room. It has a ping-pong table, pool table, a couple of video game machines and even some exercise equipment. I never saw anything like it."

Eric said, "Wow! Josh, you should invite us over some time."

Brett shouted, "Yeah!"

Josh laughed, "I'll talk to my mom and dad. I know they would love for you to come over."

They left the movie theater at ten fifteen. Brett said, "How about heading over to Mickey D's for a bite."

Scott and Eric agreed but Josh said, "Would you guys mind if I skipped Mickey D's and head home? That is, if you don't mind Scott. This is my first night out, and I don't want to get back too late. I don't even know if I have a curfew. And I know my brothers will be waiting for me to give them a report."

Scott said, "Actually, I agree you should get back home since it's your first night out and all. I'll take Josh home and then catch up with you guys."

When they got to Josh's home, Scott cut the engine and asked, "So did you have fun today?"

"Oh my god, I never had so much fun in my life thanks to you."

"When you went to the men's room, Eric and Brett told me they really like you. They think you're cool. They said they hoped you would hang with us all the time."

Josh laughed, "Me, cool? I don't think so."

Scott got serious and said, "Josh, I meant what I said this afternoon."

"What do you mean? You said a lot of things."

"That I want to be your friend."

"Thanks, Scott, that means so much to me."

"How about a hug before I take off?"

After the brief hug, Josh happily walked to the house. When he walked in, he heard the familiar thunder of footsteps on the stairs as Jared and Jason came running down. Their mom who was sitting in the living room with their dad yelled, "Slow down boys." Josh was then hit with a barrage of questions from the two boys.

"Well, how was it?"

"Did you have a good time?"

"Where did you go?"

"What did you do?"

"Who was there?"

As Sue and John were laughing, Josh said, "Whoa, Whoa. Give me a chance and I'll tell you. But first, I have to ask Mom and Dad something. Mom, Dad, I should have asked before I left, but what time is my curfew?"

His dad replied, "Well, let's see. You're going to be eighteen soon which means that you will be an adult, legally speaking. So since we trust you, I think we can leave it up to your own judgment, if that is okay with your mom."

Sue replied, "That's fine with me. I know you do have good judgment and won't take advantage. I would only suggest that if you know you will be back very late, let us know."

Jason slyly asked, "Does that mean we can use our judgments too?"

His dad just glared at him. "I guess not."

"Mom, Dad, you're the greatest."

Josh sat down and told them about his evening, the video games, bowling and the movie. He said, "You should have seen me trying to heave that heavy bowling ball down the lane. On my first try, I guess my feet got tangled and I went flying in the air and landed on my butt. The dumb ball also went flying and it landed in the lane next to ours. I got up rubbing my sore butt and Scott, Brett and Eric were rolling around on the floor laughing their heads off. The people in the other lane were laughing and so were about twenty other people who saw what happened. They must have been laughing for at least ten minutes." His mom, dad, Jared and Jason were now laughing *their* heads off and Jared and Jason, like Josh's friends, were rolling on the floor.

After a couple minutes, the laughter lessened a bit. Jason went running out of the room and came right back holding a bottle of liniment. He went over to Josh and said while still laughing, "Josh, drop our drawers and I'll rub your sore butt with liniment." The roars of laughter began all over again.

"Oh, I almost forgot. Brett and Eric wanted to know about how I got here. Scott told me I didn't have to, but I told him I had to. So I told them the whole sorry story of my past, and guess what. I didn't shed one tear. And I was the only there who didn't. Mom, Dad, Jared, Jason . . . my past is no longer part of my life. I can't wait to call Mark tomorrow to tell him."

"The best part about tonight was I felt like a normal person, like I do when I'm with you. I'm no longer afraid of anything. Scott, Eric and Brett treated me like a normal person, like a friend, like I was one of them. It feels really good to know I have friends. By the way Jared and Jason, Scott told Eric and Brett that next week you and your friends are coming with us." Jared and Jason were beaming.

Sue said, "Josh, why don't you invite your friends over some time. We would love to meet them."

"Mom, Scott told them about our yard and the game room and they did ask me to invite them over."

"Good. You work it out with them. Maybe we can have a barbecue or something."

The next day, Sunday, Josh called Bobby's parents. "Hello, Mrs. Andrews, this is Josh."

Mrs. Andrews happily responded, "Oh, Josh, it's so good to hear from you. We can't thank you enough for what you did for Bobby."

"You don't have to thank me. I didn't do that much. All I did was play with him. I had a great time."

"You don't understand how much you did for him. We tried everything to get him out of his shell. It's as if Bobby was afraid of everything and everybody outside this house. We tried to put him into a pre-K program, but when we took him there, he became hysterical when we said we were leaving. So we couldn't even enroll him. As I told your mom, we've been sending him to a child psychologist and it didn't help at all. You . . . you worked a miracle." Josh could hear Mrs. Andrews softly crying.

"Thank you Mrs. Andrews. The reason I called is to ask you when it's a good day for me to come over to see Bobby."

Mrs. Andrews nearly shouted, "Any day, any time. Bobby's been talking about you all week. Every day, he asks us when is Josh coming."

"I would have called sooner, but our court petitions were heard on Friday so I was pretty much out of it until it was finally over." Mrs. Andrews asked Josh how it went in court. "Our petitions were granted and I am now legally the son of Sue and John Brennan. I am so happy about that."

"Congratulations! I am so happy for you. I know Sue, John and the boys are happy as well. Now, if you're sure you have the time you can come here anytime. Whenever you want."

"Do you have any plans today?"

"No, we have nothing planned. We are somewhat restricted in what we can do and where we can go because of Bobby's fears."

"Well, it's now a little past 10:00 a.m. How about in an hour or so? My mom told me where you live."

"That's perfect. Bobby is going to be thrilled. And we expect you to stay for lunch."

When he was done with his call, Josh told his family that he was going to Bobby's house. He asked Jared and Jason if they wanted to go.

Jared said, "Oh no! We were just going to ask you if you wanted to come with us to Scott's and David's house. They just called and asked if the three of wanted to go with them to a softball game. Their father is playing. We told them we would go."

Jason asked, "Can't we call and tell them we can't go?"

Josh said, "Jason, that wouldn't be cool. It's my fault. I should have checked with you guys before I called Mrs. Andrews. From now on, the three of us have to be better coordinated."

Josh told his mom and dad, "I'll be having lunch with Bobby and his parents. I guess I'll be back about three o'clock or so. Or sooner, if Bobby wears me out."

When Josh arrived at Bobby's house, Bobby was out in front with his mom and dad. He got out of his car and Bobby came running toward Josh shouting. "Uncle Josh, Uncle Josh . . . you're here."

When he got near, Josh squatted and Bobby put his arms around Josh's neck and hugged him tight. "You kept your promise. I love you, Uncle Josh."

"And I love you, Bobby. We're going to have a lot of fun today. Come on, let me say hello to your mom and dad." Josh put Bobby on his shoulders and walked to the parents.

After their hellos, Mr. Andrews said, "Josh, thank you so much for coming and for what you've already done for our son. Since last Sunday, he's like a different person. He seems more energetic and outgoing. And somewhat happier. You, Josh, are a miracle worker."

A blushing Josh said, "Mr. and Mrs. Andrews, I didn't do that much and I don't deserve any credit."

Mrs. Andrews added, "Oh yes, you do. And since Bobby proclaimed you to be his uncle, we happily welcome you as one of our family." She laughed as she said that.

"There is one thing though. Mr. and Mrs. seems so formal. Please use our given names, Ann and Matt. Come inside and we'll give you a tour of the house."

After the brief tour, Ann said, "Bobby, why don't you show your Uncle Josh your room and then we'll have lunch."

"Yeah," shouted a very excited Bobby. "Come on, Uncle Josh, Let's go." He grabbed Josh's hand and up they went.

They returned twenty minutes later and Bobby said, "Uncle Josh showed me how to play some games and I won. Yay!"

After lunch, Josh asked Ann and Matt, "My dad and mom told me there was a park around here and that it has some things to play with. Do you know about it?"

Ann replied, "Oh yes, it's only a couple of blocks from here. They have a slide, swings, rocking horses, a trampoline and a sort of Jungle Jim contraption."

Matt added, "We've taken Bobby there a couple of times, but he didn't want to try anything, he was too scared. He just sat on the horses. We couldn't get him to try the rest, not even the swings."

Josh asked, "Bobby, would you go to the park with me?"

"No, I'm scared."

"But we'll have a lot of fun. You can show me how to ride the horsey."

"Huh? You don't know how to ride a horsey?"

"No, I think I would be scared. But I wouldn't be scared if you showed me." Josh then stood up as if he was ready to leave.

"Okay, Uncle Josh, I'll show you. You don't have to be scared."

Matt whispered in Josh's ear, "Josh, you're not only a miracle worker, but you're also a psychologist." Josh laughed.

Since the park was only a couple of blocks away, Josh and Bobby walked. After the first block, Josh lifted Bobby onto his shoulders for the rest of the walk. Ann and Matt stayed behind. They got their camera out and followed the two boys, but at a distance so that the boys wouldn't see them.

When they got to the park, Bobby started to get excited and said, "There's the horseys."

Josh let him off his shoulders and Bobby grabbed Josh's hand and said, "Let's go Uncle Josh. Don't be scared." So they both got on a horsey and rocked back and forth and up and down.

Josh said, "Thanks, Bobby, now I'm not scared."

Ann and Matt had arrived and were recording the two boys.

After about ten minutes, Josh said, "Come on, Bobby," and they headed to the slide. "Let's go down the slide."

"No, I'm scared. It's too high."

Josh said, "Watch me."

He went up the steps to the slide, sat down and came swooshing down. He did it one more time and on the way down he yelled, "Whoa, this is fun."

He went over to Bobby and said, "That is so much fun. Try it."

"But suppose I fall?"

"You won't fall, because I'll be here to catch you. Come on." So Bobby climbed up and sat down.

Josh said, "Okay, I'm here waiting for you, give a little push." Bobby did and it was his turn to swoosh on down. Josh grabbed onto him when he got to the bottom.

Bobby said, "Wow, that was fun. I want to do it again." So he climbed, sat, pushed and swooshed. This time, on the way down, he shouted in delight, "Wheeee!" Ann and Matt were watching and both had tears in their eyes.

After about fifteen or twenty swooshes, Josh took Bobby to the swings and he hopped on one of them. He said, "Bobby, sit on the swing next to me." Bobby hesitantly walked to the swing and sat on it. "Now go back and forth like I'm doing."

"I'm scared, Uncle Josh."

"Just hold the rope. Here, let me help you."

He walked behind Bobby and said, "Just hold the rope. Now I'm going to push you like this." He gently pushed and Bobby's swing started to move about two feet back and forth. He pushed a little harder and the distance was about five feet back and forth.

Bobby shouted out, "Whoa, this is fun. Push me higher . . . Whoa . . . wheeee . . . this feels so good."

After about ten minutes, Josh eased up on his push. It stopped and Bobby got off. "Uncle Josh, this was even better than the slide."

Josh said, "Let's rest a little." He handed Bobby a bottle of water.

Ann and Matt stood close by. Matt, although still teary eyed, continued to record everything. Ann was softly crying.

Josh noticed a little boy, about the same age as Bobby, walking into the park with, he guessed, his parents. When they got close, Josh heard the boy say, "I want to go on the swings." He sat on one of them and his dad got behind and started to push. Josh stared briefly at the boy, then at Bobby, then at the boy again. He had an idea. "Bobby, wait here for a minute. I have to talk to that lady."

He walked to her and said, "Hello, my name is Josh, and that boy at the bench is Bobby."

"Hello, Josh. My name is Maria."

"Well, I was wondering. The two boys seem to be the same age, so I was wondering if I can bring Bobby over to meet your son. Bobby is a very shy and insecure boy. This is basically his first time playing outdoors. Bobby has never played with anyone his age. He's been afraid of everything and everybody outside his house. According to his parents, I am the only person he ever played with. I'd like to see if the two boys could hopefully end up playing with each other."

"That's a wonderful idea. You see, we are new to this area. We moved here about two weeks ago, and we don't know anyone just yet. We thought we'd have to wait until school starts for our son, Kevin, to meet kids his own age. I guess he's just the opposite of your Bobby because Kevin's a very outgoing boy. If there is anyone who can get Bobby to play, believe me it's Kevin. Are you related to Bobby?"

"No, just a family friend. I just met Bobby last week. I'm trying to help his parents and get him out of his shell. I was going to bring Bobby to the trampoline next. Do you think Kevin would want to come with us?"

"I'm sure he would. Andrew, bring Kevin over here. I want you to meet someone."

Josh went to get Bobby and when they returned, Maria introduced Andrew and Kevin to Josh. She briefly told Andrew of the conversation she had with Josh. Then Josh squatted and said, "Bobby, this is Kevin. Kevin, this is Bobby."

Kevin said, "Hi, Bobby."

Bobby hugged Josh and said nothing. Josh quickly said, "Let's go over there." He nodded to Maria.

When they got to the trampoline, Bobby asked, "What's this?"

Josh said, "It's a trampoline. I'll show you what it is." He hopped on and bounced up and down. Then he bounced and landed in a sitting position.

He said to Bobby, "This is so much fun. Let me lift you up."

"No, I'm scared Uncle Josh."

Josh jumped down and asked Maria and Andrew to give him a minute. He took Bobby aside and said, "Bobby, do you remember you said you were scared of the slide because you might fall?" Bobby nodded his head.

"And do you remember you were scared to get on the swings?" Bobby nodded again.

"I didn't let anything bad happen to you then and I won't now. I'll hold you tight like I did in the pool last week."

"But you went so high."

"Okay, we don't even have to jump. We'll just walk on it."

"Okay, Uncle Josh, I'll try."

They returned to the trampoline and Josh lifted Bobby onto it. Josh took hold of Bobby's hands and went up and down without jumping. He noticed a smile on Bobby's face and Josh said, "Isn't this fun?"

"Yeah, it is. Go higher, Uncle Josh." They did, and Bobby started screaming in delight.

Josh bounced them to a stop and Bobby asked, "Why did you stop. I want to do it more."

"We will, but wait here."

Josh went to the edge and asked, "Kevin, do you want to come up?"

Kevin shouted, "Yeah."

So the three of them held hands and bounced and bounced, higher and higher. Both boys were screaming and shouting in glee.

Josh then said, "Watch this."

He landed in a sitting position and told the two boys to do that next.

After a couple minutes of more bounces and screams, Josh loosened his hands that were holding Bobby's and Kevin's, then put Bobby's hand into Kevin's. Now the two young boys, with both hands clasped into each other's, were bouncing alone. Josh was watching carefully and when he thought they were getting too close to the edge, he took their elbows and bounced them toward the center. Then the most remarkable thing happened. The two boys got closer to one another and all of a sudden they were actually hugging while bouncing. Josh was thrilled when he saw this. Finally, Josh noticed the two boys were tiring so he went to them, took their elbows and bounced them to a halt.

When they got off the trampoline, Josh noticed Bobby's parents standing there. He also noticed they both had tears flowing from their eyes. When Bobby saw them, he went running to them, "Mommy, Daddy, did you see me on the trampoline?" They hugged their precious child and told him how proud they were and that he was absolutely wonderful. Josh then introduced Ann and Matt to Maria, Andrew and Kevin.

They all went to a picnic table where Ann opened a bag which contained snacks and bottled water.

Matt said to Maria and Andrew, "This is the first time Bobby has played with anyone, let alone someone his own age. And it's all because of Josh. We call him our miracle worker."

Ann added, "I almost couldn't believe what I was seeing on the trampoline, and when they bounced while hugging, I couldn't stop crying."

Maria said, "As I told Josh, we're new to this area so Kevin doesn't know anyone his age. Maybe he and Bobby could become friends. Let's exchange contact information and keep in touch."

Ann added, "We would like nothing better than for them to become friends. Bobby needs that so badly. I'm sure Josh would help facilitate this."

Josh replied, "I would be happy to."

Ann said, "Maria, why don't I call you tomorrow and we can plan something."

"Yes, in fact why don't come to our house soon for dinner."

"Perfect. We'll set it up tomorrow."

Bobby and Kevin, holding a rubber ball about twelve inches in diameter, came running up to them. Bobby said, "Come on Uncle Josh, we want to play."

Kevin pleaded, "Yeah, come on, Uncle Josh."

Matt laughingly said, "Josh, it looks like you've been adopted into another family. Now you have three families."

The two boys each took one of Josh's hands and went running to an open field. Andrew said, "'Uncle Josh?' I thought Josh said he was a friend of the family."

Matt laughed and said, "Well, Bobby sorta adopted Josh as his uncle, and I guess Kevin also adopted him."

For over an hour, all four parents watched the three boys playing in the field, throwing and kicking the ball to each other. Kevin kicked the ball rather hard when Josh wasn't looking and he went sprawling to the ground. He just lay there in exhaustion. The two younger boys went running to him and attacked Josh. All three were rolling around on the ground. Bobby and Kevin, on top of Josh, were yelling and screaming in joy. Josh then started tickling the boys and both squealed in laughter. After twenty minutes of jostling and tickling, Josh stopped and yelled out, "I give up, I give up. You win."

The boys mercifully let Josh up. "That's enough. I have to rest. You two wore me out. Go get the ball and return it."

Josh walked back to the parents and Bobby and Kevin went running to retrieve the ball. When Josh got to the picnic table, he plopped down on the bench and said, "Oh my god, I am pooped. I think I'll sleep for a week." The parents laughed at Josh's plight. Bobby and Kevin came walking to them and amazingly each had an arm around the other's shoulder. There was a surprised, but happy look on Ann's and Matt's faces and tears came from Ann's eyes.

Bobby said, "Mommy, Daddy, Kevin wants me to go to his house tomorrow to play. Can I go?"

Ann and Matt were so shocked that they sat there in disbelief with their mouths agape as did Josh.

"Well, can I go?" Finally, both parents snapped out of their shock. Ann looked at Maria and Andrew with a questioning look.

Maria said, "It's fine with us."

Bobby pleaded, "Mommy, Daddy, can I go?"

Ann said, "Of course honey, you can go. I think that it would be wonderful." She turned to Maria, "I'll call you later for the details."

"Excellent."

It was now a little past 4:00 p.m. As Ann, Matt, Josh and Bobby walked back to their home, Bobby kept repeating how much fun he had on the horsey, the slide, the swing and the trampoline. He also said he couldn't wait to go to Kevin's house tomorrow. When Bobby was done with his raving about the day, Matt said, "Josh, there is no way you can convince me that you don't work miracles." Josh blushed while Ann and Matt laughed. Matt then took Josh aside and told Ann and Bobby he had to talk to Josh.

When they were alone, Matt said, "Seriously, Josh, if you hadn't come along, I don't know what we would have or could have done for Bobby. We tried everything including a child psychologist. Ann and I thought Bobby would never overcome his fears. We were so afraid for his future." Matt had tears in his eyes. "You were a godsend in our eyes. You are a very special person, and our thanks is not enough. Just know that if there is ever anything we can do for you, let us know. Ann and I will always be grateful for what you have done, and we'll always be indebted to you."

When they rejoined Ann and Bobby, Josh told them he had to go home. Bobby jumped into Josh's arms, "Thank you, Uncle Josh. I love you so much. When can you come again? I want you to."

"I love you too, Bobby. How about next Saturday morning?" He looked at a smiling Ann and Matt when he asked that, and they nodded. "And we can ask your new buddy Kevin to come with us. Ask him when you see him tomorrow. I'll call you during the week. Okay?"

"Yeah, don't forget, Uncle Josh."

"I won't."

When he finally got home, he went to the living room and plopped on the sofa, hands and arms stretched out. His mom, dad, Jared and Jason just stared at him.

Jason finally said, "Josh, you look shot."

Jared added, "Yeah, it looks like you were run over by a train."

Josh agreed, "Yeah, and it feels like I got run over by a train. Jason, go get the liniment. I'm sore all over. I think I need the whole bottle." Of course his family got a big laugh over that.

Josh then proceeded to tell his family about his day, the slide, the swings, the trampoline and the playing in the open field. He also told them how Bobby overcame his fears of something new to him.

He told them about Kevin and how Bobby enjoyed playing with him. Josh said, "You should have seen it. When I put Bobby's hand in Kevin's, they were bouncing together without me. Then all of a sudden, they were hugging each other while bouncing. It was remarkable. I think Bobby has overcome *all* his fears. He is even going over to Kevin's house tomorrow to play. I think they are going to become good friends."

Sue then said, "That is so wonderful. I feel so happy for Ann and Matt, and, of course, for Bobby."

John added, "Josh, you should feel very proud of yourself. You did what no one else was able to do."

Josh replied, "Well, I am very happy for the way things worked out for Bobby. Whoa, I almost forgot to tell you that I became an uncle."

Jason and Jared both cried out, "An uncle!"

"Yeah, when I got there, Bobby started calling me Uncle Josh and then Kevin also started calling me Uncle Josh. Both Bobby's parents and Kevin's parents said I was now part of their families."

Josh's dad, with a smile, said, "Josh, your family is growing by leaps and bounds. You now have two brothers and two nephews. And you also have three families."

Jason cried out, "Hey, that's not fair. I want to be an uncle too."

Jared chimed in, "Yeah, me too."

Josh replied, "I'm going to Bobby's next Saturday morning. Jared, Jason, I hope both of you can come. I need all the help I can get with two energetic and wild five-year-olds."

After Jared and Josh said they wanted to go, Josh said, "I'll introduce you as Uncle Jared and Uncle Jason. I am positive they will adopt both of you."

Jason yelled out, "All right."

Their mom then said, "Now that the uncle business is all settled, dinner will be in about an hour."

Everyone but Josh got up. Jared looked at him and said, "Aren't you going upstairs?"

Josh replied, "I would if I could get up. Bros, help me up." As they did, everyone (except Josh) was laughing.

The very next day, Monday, Josh registered at the community college and he did select the same courses that Scott had so they would be able to commute together. During the rest of the summer, Josh worked at his landscaping job and worked around the house and yard doing chores. He spent a lot of time with Jared and Jason and always included them when he was doing some social things with Scott, Eric, Brett and Rob (whom he met when he returned from his trip). Josh also visited Judge and Mrs. Harding a few times, as he did with Mr. Stafford, Mr. Conway and Ms. Marlowe. He also communicated almost daily with Mark, either by phone or computer. He reserved every Saturday morning for Bobby and Kevin, and *Uncle* Jared and *Uncle* Jason always went with him to play with the young boys. It was a busy summer for Josh but he loved every moment of his new life.

One evening, the Brennan family was sitting on the patio enjoying the warm weather. They began talking about things in general when his mom said, "Josh, it looks like you are in deep thought."

Josh's mood was somewhat pensive. "Mom, I was just thinking about all the things that has happened to me since I came to your house, and of the people who helped me, starting with you, dad, Jared and Jason. I shudder when I think where I would be without the four of you. Then I think about Mr. Stafford, Mr. Conway, Ms. Marlowe and Judge Harding. I think a lot about Mark and Scott. I think about all of you and how much you did for me. I've got to figure out a way to give back and help other people eventually."

Josh stopped and looked up staring at the stars. He chuckled. Jared asked what was so funny. Josh said, "I was thinking about Clarence."

Looking up at the stars, he said, "You know, Clarence, it really is . . . It's a wonderful life."

Epilogue

Twenty years later

After completing two years at the community college, Josh had long talks with both his dad, Mr. Stafford and Judge Harding before declaring his major at the university. He had no difficulty in making his decision. Josh had been very much influenced by Mr. Stafford's handling of his case, and seeing how and why he wanted to help a desperate young person. He wanted to follow the same path.

He majored in Political Science at the University and graduated with honors. When he decided he wanted to get a law degree, his parents were elated, as was Mr. Stafford, who in reality thought of and treated Josh as a son. He advised and guided Josh along the way as did Judge Harding. Mr. Stafford made a deal with Josh. He would pay for the tuition at the law school, and in return he wanted Josh to join his firm for a minimum of three years upon receiving his degree and passing the bar exam. Upon completion of those three years, Josh could decide whether to stay on or move on. Mr. Stafford then shocked Josh by telling him that if things worked out, Josh could take over the practice when he retired. He explained that he had three children and none of them had been interested in the law as each followed a different career path. He also told Josh that Daniel Conway was leaving his firm to relocate in another state. Of course, Josh accepted the offer.

Now at the age of thirty-seven, he did, indeed, take over the practice as Mr. Stafford retired two years ago. The practice was thriving but Josh did *pro bono* cases as the need warranted. In his desire to "pay back," he also spent time at juvenile centers for troubled teens, counseling youngsters.

He is married now with two beautiful children, a now six-year-old boy and a four-year-old girl. He met his beautiful wife while both were in law school and now they are soul mates. He cherishes his time with his family and never lets his practice or volunteer work take away from the time spends with his wife and children.

Throughout the twenty years, he remained close to his parents and two brothers and they saw each other very often. He maintained his friendship with Scott, now a computer programmer, and they were now very close friends. He often communicated with Judge Harding and visited him from time to time as he did with Jennifer Marlowe. He also kept in close touch with his "guardian angel" Mark, and at Josh's insistence, Mark did fly in once a year to visit with Josh and his family. He also stayed in contact with little Bobby and Kevin. Both were now high school teachers at the same school and are the closest of friends. Bobby also became the school's swim coach.

Jared, now thirty-five years of age, is happily married with four children, two girls and two identical twin boys. After majoring in Finance in college, he joined his dad's investment firm. He is now his dad's partner and will take over the firm when John retires.

Jason majored in Theater Arts in college and also took singing, dancing and acting lessons since he developed a passion for Broadway. And that was his goal—Broadway. When he knew he was ready for the big time, he moved to New York City and began the cattle call rounds while working as a waiter. At these cattle calls, hundreds of would-be Broadway stars would line up and when it came their turn to perform they would get only thirty seconds, so the odds were against all of them.

Two months into the cattle calls, Jason, along with a group of friends, went to a night club where anyone in the audience was invited to sing. At the urging of his group, Jason went up to perform. Jason decided to give the audience the full treatment so he sang verses of a variety of genres—ballads, jazz, soul, country, and even rap. He also included a dance routine from the very start, the audience was cheering, whistling and shouting their approval. Jason fed into this reaction and he got better and better. Finally, he sang a very dramatic song. He was so into the song that tears were falling from his eyes. With a standing ovation, the audience went wild as Jason exited the stage.

Before he got to the table where his friends were sitting, a gentleman who looked to be in his fifties asked Jason if he could speak with him. It turned out he was a producer of Broadway shows. He told Jason he never saw a performance like his. He said he was producing a new show that would open in six months or so. He said he was looking for a new face and he thought he found one tonight. At the young age of twenty-four, Jason did get the lead in that show. Of course, his mom, dad, Jared, Josh, Mark, David, Scott and all their wives attended opening night of the show. They also attended the Tony Awards, and they joyfully watched Jason win a Tony as the Best Male Lead Performer in a musical. Jason became a big star. Now at the age of thirty-three, Jason is happily married with a two-year-old son. Since his first show, Jason starred in three more musicals. In between shows, he gives concerts at major venues throughout the country. He recently recorded a CD album which achieved the Platinum level in sales. He dedicated the album to his mom, dad, Jared and Josh.

Sue and John Brennan are now fifty-eight years old and both thought they would retire when they turned sixty-two. With their nest empty of their children, they are enjoying being grandparents to seven beautiful grandchildren. They spend much of their time with them and always jump at the chance to baby sit. Since Jason lived in New York City, Sue and John flew up at least four times each year to visit him. When Josh finished law school at age twenty-five, he contacted all those who helped him along the way for a reunion. Attending were Josh, his mom and dad, Jared and Jason, William Stafford, Daniel Conway, Jennifer Marlowe, Judge Harding, Mark, Scott, David, Bobby and Kevin. After greeting and thanking everyone at the door, Josh went to the microphone, thanked them for attending and said, "My little bro Jason asked if he can say a few words, about what I don't know. Jason."

Jason approached the microphone and said, "Thank you Josh." Addressing the group, he continued, "As you may know, I have more than a slight interest in music. So for this occasion, I wrote a little something which I would like to sing for you. Since this is my first attempt at writing music, I hope you won't be too disappointed. So here goes."

This is a song I sing to you
and in this song each word is true
To our mom, so full of love
You're our rock, sent to us from up above
You nurtured us, then showed us how to grow
and learn
Always there for us at every turn
So what we say is very true
From each of us mom, we love you
To our dad, so wise and strong
In our eyes, you could do no wrong
You are someone we'd want to be
You're a hero for all we three
So what we say is very true
From each of us dad, we love you
To Jared, my older bro
You guided me so I could grow
You cared for me through thick and thin
A better bro, you could not have been
So what we say is very true

From each of us Jared, we love you
To Josh, my oldest bro
How much we love you, you'll never know
You came to us and made our family whole
And to share our love was your only goal
So what we say is very true
From each of us Josh, we love you
And to all our friends
You helped us way above and beyond
And now between us is an unbreakable bond
Because of all of you, our family is complete
What you did for us was no small feat
So what we say is very true
Mr. Stafford, Mr. Conway, Ms. Marlowe, Judge
Harding, Scott, David, Mark, Bobby, Kevin
The Brennan family will always love you

As Jason was singing, there were tears flowing from his eyes and each person in the room was wiping away their tears as Jason sang. Jason went to his parents and gave them a hug. He then went to Jared and Josh and emotionally said, "Group hug." The entire Brennan family then went to each of their friends with hugs for all.

This became an annual tradition and all those attending came with their families. Once a year, Josh would thank them individually and conclude the reunion with a toast. Each year, he would say . . .

"It's a Wonderful Life."

About the Author

The author was a teacher of high school students for thirty-two years. In addition to his classroom teaching, he also served as an adviser and counselor to his students. He had counseled hundreds of students with personal problems; most of which involved their home lives and their parents.

CPSIA information can be obtained
at www.ICGtesting.com
Printed in the USA
FFHW021421170119
50181320-55127FF